I0663957

Learn Basque with Short Stories - Pernando Amezketarra

HypLern Interlinear Project
www.hyplern.com

First edition: 2025, November
Author: Gregorio de Mújica
Translation: Kees van den End
Foreword: Camilo Andrés Bonilla Carvajal PhD

Translation and interlinear formatting © 2025 Bermuda Word. All rights
reserved.

ISBN: 978-1-83425-101-1
kees@hyplern.com
www.hyplern.com

Learn Basque with Short Stories - Pernando Amezketarra

Interlinear Basque to English

Author
Gregorio de Mújica

Translation
Kees van den End

HypLern Interlinear Project
www.hyplern.com

The HypLern Method

Learning a foreign language should not mean leafing through page after page in a bilingual dictionary until one's fingertips begin to hurt. Quite the contrary, through everyday language use, friendly reading, and direct exposure to the language we can get well on our way towards mastery of the vocabulary and grammar needed to read native texts. In this manner, learners can be successful in the foreign language without too much study of grammar paradigms or rules. Indeed, Seneca expresses in his sixth epistle that "Longum iter est per praecepta, breve et efficax per exempla[1]."

The HypLern series constitutes an effort to provide a highly effective tool for experiential foreign language learning. Those who are genuinely interested in utilizing original literary works to learn a foreign language do not have to use conventional graded texts or adapted versions for novice readers. The former only distort the actual essence of literary works, while the latter are highly reduced in vocabulary and relevant content. This collection aims to bring the lively experience of reading stories as directly told by their very authors to foreign language learners.

Most excited adult language learners will at some point seek their teachers' guidance on the process of learning to read in the foreign language rather than seeking out external opinions. However, both teachers and learners lack a general reading technique or strategy. Oftentimes, students undertake the reading task equipped with nothing more than a bilingual dictionary, a grammar book, and lots of courage. These efforts often end in frustration as the student builds mis-constructed nonsensical sentences after many hours spent on an aimless translation drill.

Consequently, we have decided to develop this series of interlinear translations intended to afford a comprehensive edition of unabridged texts. These texts are presented as they were originally written with no changes in word choice or order. As a result, we have a translated piece conveying the true meaning under every word from the original work. Our readers receive then two books in just one volume: the original version and its translation.

The reading task is no longer a laborious exercise of patiently decoding unclear and seemingly complex paragraphs. What's more, reading becomes an enjoyable and meaningful process of cultural, philosophical and linguistic learning. Independent learners can then acquire expressions and vocabulary while understanding pragmatic and socio-cultural dimensions of the target language by reading in it rather than reading about it.

Our proposal, however, does not claim to be a novelty. Interlinear translation is as old as the Spanish tongue, e.g. "glosses of [Saint] Emilianus", interlinear bibles in Old German, and of course James Hamilton's work in the 1800s. About the latter, we remind the readers, that as a revolutionary freethinker he promoted the publication of Greco-Roman classic works and further pieces in diverse languages. His effort, such as ours, sought to lighten the exhausting task of looking words up in large glossaries as an educational practice: "if there is any thing which fills reflecting men with melancholy and regret, it is the waste of mortal time, parental money, and puerile happiness, in the present method of pursuing Latin and Greek[2]".

Additionally, another influential figure in the same line of thought as Hamilton was John Locke. Locke was also the philosopher and translator of the Fabulae AEsopi in an interlinear plan. In 1600, he was already suggesting that interlinear texts, everyday communication, and use of the target language could be the most appropriate ways to achieve language learning:

> ...the true and genuine Way, and that which I would propose, not only as the easiest and best, wherein a Child might, without pains or Chiding, get a Language which others are wont to be whipt for at School six or seven Years together...[3]

---

1 "The journey is long through precepts, but brief and effective through examples". Seneca, Lucius Annaeus. (1961) Ad Lucilium Epistulae Morales, vol. I. London: W. Heinemann.

2 In: Hamilton, James (1829?) History, principles, practice and results of the Hamiltonian system, with answers to the Edinburgh and Westminster reviews; A lecture delivered at Liverpool; and instructions for the use of the books published on the system. Londres: W. Aylott and Co., 8, Pater Noster Row. p. 29.

3 In: Locke, John. (1693) Some thoughts concerning education. Londres: A. and J. Churchill. pp. 196-7.

Who can benefit from this edition?

We identify three kinds of readers, namely, those who take this work as a search tool, those who want to learn a language by reading authentic materials, and those attempting to read writers in their original language. The HypLern collection constitutes a very effective instrument for all of them.

1. For the first target audience, this edition represents a search tool to connect their mother tongue with that of the writer's. Therefore, they have the opportunity to read over an original literary work in an enriching and certain manner.
2. For the second group, reading every word or idiomatic expression in its actual context of use will yield a strong association between the form, the collocation, and the context. This will have a direct impact on long term learning of passive vocabulary, gradually building genuine reading ability in the original language. This book is an ideal companion not only to independent learners but also to those who take lessons with a teacher. At the same time, the continuous feeling of achievement produced during the process of reading original authors both stimulates and empowers the learner to study[1].
3. Finally, the third kind of reader will notice the same benefits as the previous ones. The proximity of a word and its translation in our interlinear texts is a step further from other collections, such as the Loeb Classical Library. Although their works might be considered the most famous in this genre, the presentation of texts on opposite pages hinders the immediate link between words and their semantic equivalence in our native tongue (or one we have a strong mastery of).

---

1 Some further ways of using the present work include:

1. As you progress through the stories, focus less on the lower line (the English translation). Instead, try to read through the upper line, staying in the foreign language as long as possible.
2. Even if you find glosses or explanatory footnotes about the mechanics of the language, you should make your own hypotheses on word formation and syntactical functions in a sentence. Feel confident about inferring your own language rules and test them progressively. You can also take notes concerning those idiomatic expressions or special language usage that calls your attention for later study.
3. As soon as you finish each text, check the reading in the original version (with no interlinear or parallel translation). This will fulfil the main goal of this

collection: bridging the gap between readers and original literary works, training them to read directly and independently.

Why interlinear?

Conventionally speaking, tiresome reading in tricky and exhausting circumstances has been the common definition of learning by texts. This collection offers a friendly reading format where the language is not a stumbling block anymore. Contrastively, our collection presents a language as a vehicle through which readers can attain and understand their authors' written ideas.

While learning to read, most people are urged to use the dictionary and distinguish words from multiple entries. We help readers skip this step by providing the proper translation based on the surrounding context. In so doing, readers have the chance to invest energy and time in understanding the text and learning vocabulary; they read quickly and easily like a skilled horseman cantering through a book.

Thereby we stress the fact that our proposal is not new at all. Others have tried the same before, coming up with evident and substantial outcomes. Certainly, we are not pioneers in designing interlinear texts. Nonetheless, we are nowadays the only, and doubtless, the best, in providing you with interlinear foreign language texts.

Handling instructions

Using this book is very easy. Each text should be read at least three times in order to explore the whole potential of the method. The first phase is devoted to comparing words in the foreign language to those in the mother tongue. This is to say, the upper line is contrasted to the lower line as the following example shows:

Eta	Pernandok,	Marinarri	aldera	ondo	begiratu	eta	gero:
And	Pernando	Marinari	towards	well	looks	and	then

The second phase of reading focuses on capturing the meaning and sense of the original text. As readers gain practice with the method, they should be able to focus on the target language without getting distracted by the translation. New users of the method, however, may find it helpful to cover the translated lines with a piece of paper as illustrated in the image below. Subsequently, they try to understand the meaning of every word, phrase, and entire sentences in the target language itself, drawing on the translation only when necessary. In this phase, the reader should resist the temptation to look at the translation for every word. In doing so, they will find that they are able to understand a good portion of the text by reading directly in the target language, without the crutch of the translation. This is the skill we are looking to train: the ability to read and understand native materials and enjoy them as native speakers do, that being, directly in the original language.

Eta Pernandok, Marinarri aldera ondo begiratu eta gero:
And   Pernando

In the final phase, readers will be able to understand the meaning of the text when reading it without additional help. There may be some less common words and phrases which have not cemented themselves yet in the reader's brain, but the majority of the story should not pose any problems. If desired, the reader can use an SRS or some other memorization method to learning these straggling words.

Eta Pernandok, Marinarri aldera ondo begiratu eta gero:

Above all, readers will not have to look every word up in a dictionary to read a text in the foreign language. This otherwise wasted time will be spent concentrating on their principal interest. These new readers will tackle authentic texts while learning their vocabulary and expressions to use in further communicative (written or oral) situations. This book is just one work from an overall series with the same purpose. It really helps those who are afraid of having "poor vocabulary" to feel confident about reading directly in the language. To all of them and to all of you, welcome to the amazing experience of living a foreign language!

Additional tools

Check out shop.hyplern.com or contact us at info@hyplern.com for free mp3s (if available) and free empty (untranslated) versions of the eBooks that we have on offer.

For some of the older eBooks and paperbacks we have Windows, iOS and Android apps available that, next to the interlinear format, allow for a pop-up format, where hovering over a word or clicking on it gives you its meaning. The apps also have any mp3s, if available, and integrated vocabulary practice.

Visit the site hyplern.com for the same functionality online. This is where we will be working non-stop to make all our material available in multiple formats, including audio where available, and vocabulary practice.

Notes on the translation

For the most part, each word has been translated literally and you can see its translation underneath the Basque word. Occasionally, when we thought it wouldn't be clear from context what a phrase meant or when the individual words are only used as a set phrase and never in isolation (think of the French parce que or et cetera in English), we've provided an idiomatic translation as well. These appear underneath the literal translations.

It's not imperative that you understand every single word or grammatical meaning, at least not at first, as you read through the story you will start to pick up on the patterns and things will begin to clear up. Ideally, you would read through the book several times -- after each repetition you should find that you have to rely on the literal and idiomatic translations less and less.

In this Basque translation specifically, there are a few styles we've used to try to make it easier to piece together. Because of how different Basque word order is from English and most other commonly studied languages, it can be difficult to piece together a meaningful translation from the individual parts. Here are a few common patterns you'll see in the English translation which should hopefully help you make sense of the texts.

Words with a hyphen

Generally, when a translation has a hyphen, that means that it modifies the following word. For example:

comes-that / (a) mythology

This is actually *a mythology that comes*. Looking at the full sentence:

Basque / Mythology / from prehistory / comes-that / (a) mythology / is

... we get "Basque Mythology is a mythology that comes from prehistory."

Another example is:

seeing-of / way

This should be translated as *way of seeing*.

Words with parentheses

In Basque, the case ending is usually only attached to the last word in the phrase, the other words are in what is known as mugagabe, literally "without ending". Sometimes the words in parentheses are just a hint to make the meaning of the phrase in English a bit clearer, but often it's because the case wasn't marked until the end of the phrase but it makes more sense to place it up front in English. Let's look at some examples:

(in) her / inside
The "in" case is attached to "inside" (*barnean*), but it is clearer to put it up front in English.

(the) Sun / Grandmother / and / Moon / Grandmother / gods
The definte article "the" is actually part of "gods" (*jainkoak*).

explanation(s) / and / answer(s) / all
The plural marker is on the last word "all" (*guztiak*).

Notes on Basque Grammar

Word order

Word order in Basque is quite different from English. Often times the verb comes at the end of the sentence and Basque is sometimes called an SOV (Subject-Object-Verb) language, however this order is not fixed.

Generally, the most important information will come before the verb and whatever is being stressed comes directly before the verb. If it's the verb itself that is being stressed, *egin* (do) is added after the verb so that it can receive the focus of the sentence. For synthetic verbs (verbs which have their own conjugation), we can also place 'ba' in front of the verb. So *dakit* (I know) from the verb *jakin* (to know) becomes *badakit*.

Another confusing bit for English speakers is how relative clauses are formed. In Basque, you often add an *n* to the main verb of the phrase, unless it already ends in an *n* (such as past tense verbs), and this converts that phrase into something of an adjective. For example, look at this phrase: Gizona joan da. *The man has gone* ...If we want to say "The man who/that has gone" we need to turn "joan da" into an adjective: Joan den gizona *Has gone-that man* (The man who has gone)

Many times you'll find a series of phrases like this stringed together, often with cases added to them (*joan den gizonarekin* - with the man who has gone) and it can get a bit confusing, but if you take your time and read through the sentence a couple times and check out our literal and idiomatic translations, you should be able to piece them together. And as you read through the book and its individual stories multiple times, it'll get easier!

Cases

Like many languages, Basque has a system of cases. There are quite a few cases, but fortunately they are very regular. Each case generally has four forms, singular, plural, *mugagabe*/indeterminate, and proper nouns. The singular, *mugagabe*, and proper noun forms may add an 'e' if the last letter in the stem is a consonant. Also, it's generally only the last word in a phrase which gets the case, the rest are left without any ending. So to say "with the beautiful man", we only need to put the last word in "norekin": *gizon ederrarekin* (and not *gizonarekin ederrarekin*). Let's look at a chart of the most common cases and then discuss what exactly each case is used for:

	Singular	Plural	Mugagabe	Proper Nouns
nor	-a	-ak	--	--
nork	-ak	-ek	-(e)k	-(e)k
nori	-ari	-ei	-(r)i	-(r)i
noren	-aren	-en	-(r)en	-(r)en
norentzat	-arentzat	-entzat	-(r)entzat	-(r)entzat
norekin	-arekin	-ekin	-(r)ekin	-(r)ekin
nola	-az	-ez	-(e)z / -(e)taz	-(e)z
non	-(e)an	-etan	-(e)tan	-(e)n
nora	-(e)ra	-etara	-(e)tara	-(r)a / -era
nondik	-(e)tik	-etatik	-(e)tatik	-tik / -dik
nongo	-(e)ko	-etako	-(e)tako	-ko / -go

nor

This is the neutral case. It is generally translated as *the* but sometimes it makes more sense to translate it as *a*. Direct objects and subjects of transitive verbs take this case.

nork

Also known as the ergative case. This shows the subject of a transitive verb. In Basque, you mark the subject of the verb, not the direct object (accusative) like you would in German or Russian.

nori

The dative case. Shows the indirect object, often translated as *to* in English. It's also commonly used with non-transitive verbs, similar to Spanish: *me gusta → gustatzen zait* "she/he/it is pleasing to me" (I like it/him/her) *se me ha muerto el gato → katua hil zait* "to me the cat has died" (my cat has died)

noren

The genitive case. Shows possession, similar to English *'s* or *of*.

norentzat

The benefactive case. Almost always translated as *for*. It shows who something is for, who or what it was intended for.

norekin

The comitative case. Generally can be translated as *with* when talking about company (being with someone) and not what you used to do something, which is our next case.

nola

The instrumental case. This shows what you use to do something. It's also used with languages to say *in X language*, eg. *euskaraz* (in Basque) or *ingelesez* (in English). Another use is with the meaning of *about*, eg. *zutaz hitz egin* (to talk about you).

non

The inessive case. This talks about where and when. It usually means *in*, *at*, or *on*, though it's often left untranslated in English when talking about times.

nora

The allative case. This case answers the question "to where?" You'll generally translate it as *to* when referring to a direction, going someplace.

nondik

The ablative case. This case answers the questions "from where?" and "since when?" and can usually be translated as *from* or *since*. It also can be used to show which way you are going, in which case it usually takes the meaning of *through* or *by*.

nongo

This is another genitive case, but is used for places. This case can be a bit confusing and it can be difficult to decide which one to use, but in general we use this case when talking about a place or time, such as *goizeko hamarrak* (ten of the morning, 10am) or *kotxeko giltzak* (keys of the car, car keys). It's also frequently used to talk about where a person or thing is from, eg. *Bilboko taberna bat* (a "Bilbao" bar, a bar in Bilbao) or *Nafarroakoa naiz* (I am of Navarre, I'm from Navarre).

Verbs

The Basque verb system is infamous for being complex. It's not really that complex once you start to get familiar with it, but there are a lot of forms and it can take a long time to get used to them. I recommend finding a Basque verb chart (such as this one from Wikipedia) and either printing it out or keeping it handy on your phone/computer. Luckily, most verbs in Basque aren't usually conjugated, they use an auxiliary verb along with the participle.

The participle has three main forms, the perfect stem (*egin, hartu, ikusi*), which is the dictionary form, the future stem (*egingo, hartuko, ikusiko*), and the imperfect stem (*egiten, hartzen, ikusten*). These combine with the auxiliary verb to give us a flexible range of tenses.

The auxiliary verb has a few different types, depending on what kind of verb it is. Verbs are generally split into transitive verbs, whose subject takes the ergative/nork case, and intransitive verbs, whose subject takes the absolutive/nor case. Intransitive verbs take the auxiliary verb *izan* and transitive verbs take the auxiliary *ukan*. Let's look at the intransitive verbs first.

Intransitive Verbs

nor

These are your standard intransitive verbs. They have a subject but no object, such as *joan* (to go), *etorri* (to come), and *jaiki* (to get up). The auxiliary verb only tells us the subject, ie. who's performing the action. The *nor* auxiliary verb looks like this in the present tense:

naiz	(I) am
da	(he/she/it) is
gara	(we) are
zara	(you sg) are
zarete	(you pl) are
dira	(they) are

nor-nori

These verbs have a subject and an indirect object, but no direct object. We don't have many of these kinds of verbs in English, but they are more common in Basque. If you know some Spanish, many of these verbs should feel familiar to you. First, let's look at the present tense forms:

nor	nori
natzai	t
zai	o
gatzaiazki	gu
zatzaizki	zu
zatzaizki+te	zue
zaizki	e

The most common forms you will see are the *zai-* and *zaizki-* forms. These are the third person singular and plural forms. The form on the left tells us the subject (the *nor*) and the form on the right tells us the indirect object (the *nori*). An example might help clear this up:

gustatzen zatzaizkit
be pleasing / you are to me (I like you)

...*gustatu* is the verb *to be pleasing, to like*. We can see that the subject is *you* because of the *zatzaizki-* (you) form. We can tell who the indirect object is from the *-t* (to me) form. It can be a bit confusing at first, but once you get used to it, it's interesting just how much information can be put into one little verb!

Transitive Verbs

nor-nork

These are your standard transitive verbs. They have a subject and an object, verbs like *ikusi* (to see), *erosi* (to buy), and *jakin* (to know). The auxiliary verb tells us who the subject is, ie. who's performing the action, and who/what the object is, ie. who's receiving the action. Here's the *nork* auxiliary verb in the present tense (the left side is the object/*nor* and the right side is the subject/*nork*):

nor	nork
nau	t
du	--
gaitu	gu
zaitu	zu
zaituzte	zue
ditu	(z)te

The most common forms you will see are the du/ditu forms. The "z" only shows up in the forms ending in -tu, giving you *ikusi gaituzte* (they saw us), *ikusi zaituzte* (they saw you), and *ikusi dituzte* (they saw them). The other forms (naute, dute, zaituztete) add "te" directly. Let's analyze a few examples to see how the system works:

etxea ikusi duzu
the house / seen / it you have (I saw/have seen the house)

...*du-* tells us that the object is 3rd person singular (referring to the house) and *-zu* that the subject is *you*.

ikusi zaitut
seen / you I have (I saw/have seen you)

...*zaitu-* tells us the object is 2nd person singular (you) and *-t* that the subject is *I*.

ikusi ditu
seen / them he has (he saw/has seen them)

...*ditu-* tells us the object is 3rd person plural (them) and the lack of ending -- shows us the subject is *he/she/it*.

nor-nori-nork

These verbs contain quite a bit of information, they have a subject, an indirect object, and a direct object. These are often verbs of giving, showing, and telling, like *esan* (to say), *eman* (to give), and *erakutsi* (to show). Let's look at the present tense forms:

	t/da	t
	o	-
di(zki)	gu	gu
	zu	zu
	zue	zue
	e	te

The *t/da* just means that if there's anything after it, the *t* changes into *da*. So we say *esan dit* (he/she told me) but *esan didazu* (you told me). Here are a couple examples:

mutilek esango dit
the boy / will tell / it to me (the boy will tell me)

...*di-* tells us that the object is 3rd person singular, *-t-* tells us that *I* am the indirect object, and the empty ending tells us that the subject is 3rd person singular, the boy.

argazkiak erakutsi dizkizut
pictures / shown / them to you I have (I showed/have shown you the pictures)

...*dizki-* tells us that the object is plural (picture*s*), *-zu-* tells us that the indirect object is *you*, and *-t* tells us the subject is *I*.

giltzak eman dizkidate
keys / given / them to me they have (they gave/have given me the keys)

...*dizki-* tells us we have a plural object (the keys), we have *-da-* instead of *-t-* because it's not the end of the word and it tells us that *I* is the indirect object, and lastly *-te* tells us that the subject is 3rd person plural *they*.

Negative Sentences

Negative sentences are formed with the word *ez* (no). When we negate a sentence, the order changes a bit, generally sending the participle to the end of the phrase:

Galtzak eman dizkidate → *Ez dizkidate galtzak eman*

Etxea ikusi duzu → *Ez duzu etxea ikusi*

Final Notes

If you are new to studying Basque, we hope these tips help you get a better grasp on Basque word order better and make the cases more accessible. This is by no means a comprehensive grammar of the language, but we hope it's enough to get you started! If you have any questions about the text or the translation, please get in touch, we'd be happy to answer your questions. We hope you enjoy learning Basque and learning about the incredible world of Basque mythology!

Table of Contents

ETXE-GAINEKO ZENTSOAK

ETXE-GAINEKO ZENTSOAK
Above the house   Censuses
  On the house   Taxes

Halako batean, Amezketako herri-agintariak joan
Such   in one   (the) Amezketako   public authorities   go
  One day

ziren Pernandoren etxera.
did   to Pernando's   house

—Pernando —esan zioten— etxe onen gainean
Pernando   say   they did   (the) house   this   over
    they said   on

zentsoak omen daude, eta.
censuses   it is said   they are   then
taxes

—Zentsoak etxe onen gainean? —erantzun zien
Censuses   house   this   over   answer   did to them
Taxes

Pernandok—. Zaudete, zaudete pixka batean.
Pernando   Wait   Wait   little   once
    a little

Iskilara bat atera zuen ikuilutik,
Ladder   a   take out   did   from the barn
  He took out a ladder

jarri zuen etxe-gainera   igo   ahal izateko   eran,
put   did   house-against   climb could to be   they were
  put it against the house   so they could climb

eta esan zien:
and say   did to them

—Igo   jaunak, igo... Eta nire etxe gainean   ezer
Go up   gentlemen go up And my   house on top   anything

aurkitzen baduzue, hartu, Lehenago jakin izan banu
find   if you have take (it) Earlier know have if I
                              If I'd known earlier

neronek hartuko nituen;
myself   take   I did
  I'd have taken it myself

beharraren beharrez ez gera.
of need   of necessity not stay
there's no need to stay

ZAZPI JAUNGOIKO

ZAZPI   JAUNGOIKO
Seven   Gods

Praile batek, barre   egin   nahian, galdetu zion
Friar   a   laugh (emphasis) wanting to   asked   did
   A friar

Pernandori:
to Pernando

—Pernando, zenbat Jaungoiko dira?
Pernando   how many   Gods   (there) are

Eta Pernandok:
And   Pernando

—Zazpi.
Seven

—Zazpi? Nolatan gero?
Seven   How   then

—Aita, Semea eta Espiritu Santua, hiru. Hiru
Father (a) son and spirit holy three Three

pertsona diferenteak, sei. Eta Aita Eternoa, horra
persons different six And Father eternal there

zazpi.
seven

TXINGURRIEN HOTSA

TXINGURRIEN HOTSA
Ants'   Noise

Behin bi ikaslek esan zioten Pernandori:
Once   two students   say   they did   to Pernando
                        said

—Aizu,   Pernando: Marinarriko   harkaitzean   doazen
Hey   Pernando   Marinari's   rock to   they go

txingurri haiek ikusten   al   dituzu?
ants   them   seen   (question) you have

Eta Pernandok, Marinarri aldera ondo begiratu eta
And   Pernando   Marinari   towards well   looks   and

gero:
then

—Ez... urruti zegok hura nik holarrekorik ikusteko...
No   far   there is that   I   nothing like that   see

Ez   dizkiat   ikusten, baina bere hoin hotsa bai,
Not I have them   seen   but   here great noise yes

ederki aditzen diat. Zuek ez?
nicely   hear   I will You   not

—Ez, hotsik ez guk.
 No   noise   not we (hear)

—Orduan ere, zuen begietako argia niretakoa baino
 Then   also your   sight   light   mine   than
                      eyesight

hobea izan arren, nik belarriak hobeak, eh? Arre
better (past) although I   ears   better   hey Go

astotxo, arre!
little donkey   go

PITXITA

PITXITA
Little one

Bi　　　neskatxa gazte,　　apain　　eta　　lirain,
Two　　　a girl　　young　　elegant　　and　　slender
　　　　young girls

txakur txiki polit bat berekin　　zutela　　zihoazen.
dog　small　nice　one　with her　them having　went
　　a little cute dog　　　having with them

Pernandok ikusi zituan, eta esan zien:
Pernando　saw　was　and　say　did to them
　　　　saw them

—Horixe da txakurtxo polita... zer izen du?
That　is　(a) little dog　cute　what name　has

—Pitxita.
Little one

—Putzik egiten al　　du ipurdia itxita?
Blow　doing　(question) has　ass　closed
(Putzik-itxita) Does it fart　with the ass closed

HOBE IZANGO NIAN

HOBE   IZANGO   NIAN
Better   Have   I did
I would be better off

Pilota partidu ospetsu bat   **izan zen**   **behin**
Ball   match   famous   one   be   it did   once
A famous ball match   there was

Hernanin,   **gipuzkoatar**   **eta**
in Hernani   people from Gipuzkoa   and
(place in Basque country)

lapurtarren   **artean.**
people from Labourd   between

Olakoetan   gertatu hori den bezala,
Such-of-context happened that is as
As happens in such situations

dirutza handiak   **jokatu** **ziren.** **Pernandok** **ere**
fortune   large   play   did   Pernando   also
large sums of money   wagered   got

nondik   edo   handik   bi   duro   eder
from where or   from there two   duro   beautiful
                                   (historical coin)

bereganatu zituen; eta bai jokatu, eta bai galdu
obtained did and yes play and yes lost
wagered

ere.
also

Etxerakoan, Billabonako kalean zehar zihoala,
On the way home of Billabona in the street through as he went

galdetu zioten:
ask they did
they asked

—Hernanin zer berri, Pernando?
In Hernani what news Pernando

—Hernanin?
In Hernani

Irabazi duenak armonian
Won the one who has (is) in harmony
The one who has won is in harmony

beste batzuk agonian;
other some in agony
and the others in agony

nik ere joan ez banitz
I also went not if I hadn't
If I hadn't gone too

hobe izango nian.
better   have   I would
I would have been better

SARTU BITEZ!...

SARTU BITEZ!...
To Enter   Let Them
That you enter!

Pernando bazetorren Tolosatik etxera, bere asto
Pernando   was coming   from Tolosa   house to   his   donkey
home

beltza   aurrean   zuela. Olarainera iristean,   bi
black   in front of (him) having   To Olarain upon arriving two

damatxo aurkitu zituan; horiek   astoari   begira
ladies   find (him)   was   those   at the donkey   looking

jarri   ziren,   eta lokarriak min eman ez zezakion,
put   did   and   straps   pain give not it would
the straps wouldn't hurt it

isats-ondoan   zeuzkan   trapu   zaharrak   ikustean,
tail-behind   he had-that   rags   old   upon seeing
under the tail

hasi   ziran barrez.
started they did laughing

—Zu, Pernando —galdetu zioten zirikatzeagatik—
You Pernando asked they did for teasing

astoak isats-azpian daukan oihal horren kana
the donkey tail-behind has fabric such piece
under the tail

bakoitza, zenbatean saltzen duzu?
each for how much selling do you
(saldu - tzen)

—Hori bera ez dago saltzeko, andeatxo. Baina
That itself not is for sale ladies But

ori baino hobeak badauzkat denda-barruan...
that than better ones shop-inside
ones better than that one are inside the shop

Sartu bitez...
Entered let them
That you enter

Eta astoari isatsa goi-goraino jasoaz, bidea
And to the donkey the tail all the way up lifting the road

erakutsi zien.
show did to them

EULIAK ETA TXINTXARRIAK

EULIAK ETA TXINTXARRIAK
Flies   And   Bells

Amezketarren   izengoitia euliak da; alegitarrena
Those from Amezketa   nickname   flies   is   those from Alegia

berriz   txintxarriak.
on the other hand   bells

Behin batean Pernando bai omen   zioan   Alegiko
Once   in a   Pernando yes it is said was going from Alegia
Once upon a time

kalean   behera,   hosto batzuek zituen txotx bat
in the street   down   leaf   some   had   stick one
a stick with some leaves on it

eskuan   zuela.
in (his) hand   having

Alegitar   batek galdetu zion:
From Alegia   one   asked   to him-did
Someone from Alegia

—Pernando! Eskuan daramazun txotx hori
Pernando In (your) hand you are carrying stick that

euliak izutzeko al duzu?
flies to scare (question) do you

—Ez, ez. Zintzarrien mihiak isiltzeko dut.
No no The bells-of tongues to silence have

PUFFF!...

PUFFF!... Behin batean, Pernando larri zebilen
Poofff   Once   in a   Pernando   serious   he was
    Once upon a time   in trouble

bide bazter batean, eskuak sabel-gainean zituela,
road   side   in a   hands   stomach-on top   having them
    on a road side

hortzak estutu eta ostiko txikiz lurra joaz.
teeth   clenched   and   kick   small   the ground   hitting
           with small kicks

Larri zebilen, baina galtzak askatzera ez zen
Serious   he was   but   pants   to release   not   was
In trouble   did

ausartzen, jende asko zebilen eta.
daring   people   many   was   and
dare   were (there)also

Adiskide batek ikusi zuan estutasun hartan, eta
A friend   one   see   to him-did   distress   in that   and
                in that distress

esan zion:
say   to him-did

—Motel...   hortxe   bertan...   hori   guztiok   egin
Friend   right there   there   that   all of us   (emphasis)
            right there

behar   diagun   gauza   duk   eta.
need   we must   thing   you do   and
   have to do the thing   also what you do

Pernandok,   orduan,   galtzak   askatu   eta   pikotxean
Pernando   then   the pants   release   and   in a squat

  jarriaz   erantzun   zion:
positioning   answer   to him-did

—Ez,   hau   behintzat   nik   bakarrik   egin
No   this   at least   I   alone   (emphasis)

behar   dudana   duk...
have to   that I must   you do
have to do

ILARGIAREN PISUA

ILARGIAREN PISUA
The Moon's   Weight

Egun batean   Amezketako   Erretore   jauna,
Day   in one   (the) of Amezketa   rector   lord
On one day   priest

Pernandoren   adiskide   handia,   ilargiak   zenbat
to Pernando   a friend   great,   moon   how much

pisatzen   ote   zuen pentsatzen zegoen.
weighing   maybe   did   thinking   was

Hontan   Pernando albotik pasa zen, eta galdetu
At that moment   Pernando   side   pass   did   and   ask

zion erretoreak:
did   (the) priest

—Pernando: ilargia   hain handi eta ederra izanik,
Pernando   (the) moon   so   big   and beautiful   being

zenbat   pisatzen   duen   nahi   nuke   jakin.
how much   weighing   does-that want   (I) would know

Pernandok erantzun zion, galde hori erreza zela
Pernando answered him question that simple was

eta ilargiaren pisua kilo bat zela.
and the moon's weight kilo one was

—Baina horren gutxi nola? —zion erretoreak.
But   so   few   how   to him (the) priest (asked)

—Errez, jauna, ilargiak zenbat laurden ditu?
Easy   lord   moon   how many quarters has

—Lau.
Four

—Eta lau laurden ez   al   dira bada kilo bat?
And four quarters not (question) are indeed kilo one

ZAKURRA BEZELA

ZAKURRA BEZELA
    Dog   Like
Like a dog

Idia saltzera joan zen behin Tolosara, eta sanoa
Ox   to sell   go   was   once   Tolosa to   and   healthy
                  went

zen galdetu ziotenean erantzun zuena:
was   ask   when they did   answer   what you had

—Bai horixe! Zakurra bezalakoa.
Yes   exactly!   Dog   like
             (Healthy) like a dog

Erosi diote bada idi hori, eta hurrengo egunean
Buy   they say   indeed   ox   that   and   next   day-on
                                the next day

erosleak jarri du lanean: idi gizajoa,
buyers   put   has   working   (the) ox   (the) poor creature
        set   it   to work

mingaina aterata, arnaska, ezin ibilirik zen laster.
tongue   out   breathing   unable   to walk   was   soon

Jabe berria, haserre, joan zen Pernandorengana
Owner new angry go was to Pernando
went

eta eraso zion ziria sartu ziola garrasika
and attack him pin inserted he said furiously
angrily said he tricked angrily

esanaz.
claiming

—Ziria? —erantzun zion Pernandok—. Ez gizona.
Pin answer him did Pernandok No man
Trick replied dude

Zakurra bezalakoa zela esan nizun. Jarri ezazu
Dog like was say you I had Put do
I told you

zakurra lanean, eta ikusiko duzu idiak bezala
(a) dog working and will see you oxen like
to work like an ox

mingaina zeinen agudo aterako duan.
pulling how much quickly come out will

ASTOA GIZON GAINEAN

ASTOA GIZON GAINEAN
Donkey   Man   On
The donkey on the man

Taka,   taka,   bazihoan   Pernando   bere   astotxoa
There   there   leading   Pernando   his   little donkey

aurrean   zuela.   Kalera   iritsi   zen,   eta   mikeleteak
in front of having Street-to arrived he-did and the policeman
                     He arrived to the street

esan zion:
 say   to him-did
said to him

—Katea   ordaindu   behar   duzu,   Pernando.
 Chain   pay   must   you have   Pernando
Toll chain   you must pay

—Zergatik gero?
 Why   then

—Astoa   daramazulako.
 Donkey   carrying because

—Ah, eta nirerik ez eta astoarena bai?
Ah and of mine no and donkey's business yes
                              but

—Jakina ba...
Of course yes

—Nirerik ez, orduan.
Mine not then

—Ezetz.
No

—Eta bizkarrean karga badaramat ere ez?
And back-on load I-carry even no
And not if I'm carrying a load

—Ezetz bada, gizona; zurerik ez.
No if man yours no

Hori entzutean, astoa bizkarrean hartuta han
That hear-upon donkey back-on taking there
      hearing   on the back   off

joan zen   Pernando,
go was   Pernando
went

mikeletea zer egin ez zekiala utzita.
policeman what to do not knew leaving
leaving the policeman not knowing what to do

ORDAINDU ARTEKO ASTIA

ORDAINDU ARTEKO ASTIA
Pay Between Period
The time between payments

Gaixo, oso gaixo zegoen Pernando. Hartzekodun
Sick very sick was Pernando Creditor

bat etorri zitzaion ohe ondora, eta zor zizkion
one come to him-did bed to beside and debt he owed
        next to sat

diruak eskatu zizkion.
money asked from him

Pernandok, mantso mantso esan zion:
Pernando slowly slowly say him-did

—Hai zuri ordaindu arteko bizia emango balit
Oh you (I will) pay until life will give if (he) would

gure Jaungoiko maiteak! Orduantxe pozik hilko
our lord beloved Just then happy would die
        content

nitzake...
I could

Erretore jauna   zegoen,   eta   hitz haiek
Rector   sir   was (there)   and   word those
  The priest   those words

  gaixoari   entzautean, esan zion:
sick-person-to   hearing   say   to him-did
  at hearing from the patient

—Gure Jaungoikoa on-ona da, Pernando eta zure
Our   lord   good   is   Pernando and your

nahia   beteko   du   noski.   Zorrak ordaintzea
desire   fulfill   will   of course   Debts payments
                       To pay your debts

nahi du berak, eta egiteko hori bete arteko astia
want has himself and   to do that fulfill until   time
  it wants you   to fulfill that   enough

emango dizu...
will give   to you

—Ordu arteko bizia ematen   baldin badit bada,
Then   until   life giving   if   gives then
    If only until then   he gives me life

jauna,   **berorrek**
  sir   you (formal)

ez dauka nire entierroa kobraturik...
not have my burial paid
don't get my burial paid

ONETIK ERAN

ONETIK   ERAN
From There To Here

Pernandoren **behiak,** **belar** **onik** **jaten** **ez** **zuten**
Pernando's   cows   grass   good   eating   not   they had

eta, **argalak** **zeuden.** **Egun** **batean,** **behi** **zain**
and   thin   were   Day   one on   cow   watching
                                   On one day

zegoela, **auzoko** **soro** **batean** **ikusi** **zuen** **belar**
was   neighbor's field   in one   see   to him-did grass

mardul **mardula,** **eta** **hantxe** **sartu** **zituen** **ase**
lush   lush   and   right there   enter   he did   to satisfy
         very lush   let in

eta **zerbait** **gizendu** **zitezen.**
and   something   fatten   they were
      somewhat   they could

Behiak **ari** **ziren** **gogotik** **garia** **jaten,** **baina** **ona**
Cows   work   they did   eagerly   wheat   eating   but   here

non   irteten   den   baserritik   atso   bat,
then   coming out it is   from the farmhouse old woman one

deiadarka:
shouting

—Pernando!...
Pernando

—Pernando!... —erantzun zuen honek.
Pernando   replied   said this one

—Ateza hitzak behi horiek.
Drive   words   cows those
Shoo the cows out

—Ateza hitzak behi horiek.
Drive   words   cows those
Shoo the cows out

—Ez   al   duk aditzen?
Not   (question) you understand

—Ez   al   duk aditzen?
Not   (question) you understand

Atsoa,   hainbeste jardunekin   aspertu zen,
(The) old woman   so much   actions-with bored   became
                               back and forth tired

eta haserreturik esan zion:
and   angrily   say him-did
                    said to him

—Edari gaiztoak galduko al hau.
Drink   evil   lose   will this
This misfortune will ruin me

—Onetik eran —erantzun zion Pernandok.
From there to here   reply   her-did Fernando
    Same here

ESKRIBAURIK EZ ZERUAN

ESKRIBAURIK EZ ZERUAN
   No scribe   Not   In the sky
There are no scribes in heaven

Bazihoan   behin   Amezketako   Pernando,   zeukan
Was going   once   from Amezketa   Pernando   had

soineko onena jantzirik.
dress   best   wearing

Bidean   aurkitu zuen eskribaua, eta honek, hala
On the way   find   he-did (a) scribe   and this one thus

apaindua ikusirik, galdetu zion:
adorned   seeing   ask   to him-did
        having seen

—Baina Pernando, zer zabiltza horren apain?
But   Pernando what doing   so   fancy
                are you doing

—Hara jauna —erantzun zion—.   Inondik   ezin
There   sir   replied   to him-did By any means cannot
Well   he replied to him

bizi-modurik atera nuen, eta ikazkintzara joatea
no way of life   find   I did   and   to coal-making   to go

gogoratu zait.
remember   to me

—Ikazkintzara zoaz? Ez da bada ikazkintza txit
To charcoal-making   you go   Not   is   then   charcoal-making   at all

lanbide ona. Sekulan ez dut aditu zeruan
(a) profession   good   Never   not   have   heard   in heaven

ikazkinik sartu denik.
charcoal-burner   enter   that is
of a charcoal-burner entering

—Bai jauna, bai; behin sartu omen zen. Eta
Yes   sir   yes   once   entered   apparently   was   And

ikazkina zeruan ikustea gauza harrigarria
charcoal-maker   in heaven   seeing   thing   amazing

zelako eskritura egitea erabaki omen zuten.
because   writing   to do   decide   apparently   they had
they decided to write that down

Horretarako eskribaua behar ordea, eta bila eta
For that   scribe   needed   however   and   searching   and

bila **ibili** **arren,** **ez** **omen** **zuten** **aurkitu.**
looking for · walk · despite · not · apparently · they had · find
they could find one

Zerua **zeru** **denez** **geroztik,** **ez** **omen** **da** **han**
Heaven · heaven · since it is · since · not · apparently · is · there
Since heaven is heaven

eskribaurik **sartu!**
no scribe · entered

ZEREKO BEHORRAK

ZEREKO BEHORRAK
Why Cattle

Behin Pernando mendi-tontor batean,
Once Pernando mountain-summit on one
was on a mountain top

elur lapatzetan hotzak dal-dal
snow snowfall-in the midst of cold-from shivering
in heavy snow shivering from the cold

ardi zain zegoela,
sheep watching was
was watching the sheep

bere behorren bila joan zen
his of cattle looking for went did
when looking for their cattle

batek galdetu zion:
(some)one ask him-did
someone asked him

—Behorrik ikusi al duzu hemen, Pernando?
Cattle saw (question) do you here Pernando

Eta Pernandok erantzun zion:
And   Pernando   answer   him-did

—Behorrak? Zereko behorrak!...
  Cattle   Why   cattle

Ardien erdiak akabatuta
 Sheep's halves   finished
The sheep's end is done

barrutiak ezin pagatuta,
 (a) corral cannot (be) paid

ez gaude abelera txarrean geldituta.
not (we) are cattle   badly   stuck

Eguraldi horiek jarri bitza mudatuta,
 Weather   those   put   once   changed
Let that the weather changes

bestela aurki naiz ardi eta guzti
otherwise soon   will sheep and   all

akabatuta.
 (be) finished
be dead

TXERRIAREN HIL KANPAIA

TXERRIAREN   HIL   KANPAIA
(The) Pig's   Slaughter   Bell

Inori   odolkirik   ez   emateagatik
To anyone bloodletting not   for giving
So that he didn't have to give anyone some blood

bere txerria gauaz hiltzen zuen   bat   bai   omen
his   pig   at night kill   it-did   one   yes supposedly
      their pig at night killed   someone

zen Amezketan.
was   in Amezketa

Pernandok jakin zuen hori, eta erne erne egon zen
Pernando   know it-did that and alert alert be   was
Pernando found out about that   very alert   remained

txerria noiz hilko ote   zuten jakin   arte.
pig   when kill maybe they did to know until
            they might kill   until he would know

Halako batean, goizeko ordu bietan isil isilik hil
Such   in a   morning then in both silent silently killed

zuten txerri hori, eta hasi ziren erretzen...
they did | pig | that | and | started | they did | smoking
  | | | | | | roasting

Pernandok hori ikusi zuenean, joan zen arin asko
Pernando | that | saw | when he did | went | did | quickly | much
  | | | | | | very quickly

sakristauaren etxera, eta, herrian sua sala, eta
sacristan's | home | and | in the village | fire | room | and
church man's

su kanpaia jotzeko agindu zion.
fire | bell | to ring | ordered | did

Bai hala egin ere. Kanpaia zalapartaka hasi
Yes | that way | (emphasis) | also | Bell | clamorously | started

zen, amezketar guztiak esnatu eta kalera irten
did | from Amezketa | all | woken up | and | street-to | exit

ziren, eta Pernandoren atzetik han joan ziren
they did | and | of Pernando | behind | there | go | did

txerria erretzen ari ziren tokira.
pig | roasting | being | they did | to the place

Inork ikusterik nahi ez, eta herri guztiak ikusi.
Nobody | seeing | want | not | and | country | all | saw
  They wanted no one to see it   and yet everyone saw

ARDI IZUA

ARDI IZUA
Sheep Scare

Pernandok bere artaldean, ardi bat oso izua zuen:
Pernando his in the herd sheep one very scare it-did
  in his flock

esnea jaisteko kaikua eskuan zuela Pernando
milk to lower jug in (his) hand having Pernando

gerturatzen ikusi orduko, artizkunetik irten eta
approaching saw of time that from the shepherds go out and
  as soon as

han joaten zen ihesi nora nahi. Kaikuak
there to go was fleeing where want (The) bucket
  wherever it wanted

beldurtzen zuen noski.
frightened it of course

Beti bezala, halako gau batean ere, barrutiko
Always as such night in one also district's
  in such a night the corral's

horma gainetik salto eginda, joan zen Jaungoikoak
wall   over   jump   done   go   was   (the) lord

daki nora. Pernando, makila eskuan zuela, ibili
knows where Pernando (with) stick in (his) hand having walk

zen bere atzetik ordu batean, baino azkenik,
did his behind while   in a   however finally
                 for a while

aspertuta, "otsoak jango al hau" esanaz,
bored   (the) wolves eat (question) this (one) exclaiming

ardia bilatzeari utzi eta lotaratu zen.
(the) sheep searching left and fall asleep was

Goizerako artizkune inguruan izango zela
By morning shepherds place in will be was

uste zuan. Baina bai zera! ez zen etorri. Beste
think to him-did But yes that not did come Other
he thought   no way

ardiak jaitsi eta lurrera eraman zituenean,
sheep brought down and on the ground brought they did

han aurkitu zuen ardi izua, otsoak erdi
there find did (the) sheep scared (by the) wolves half

janda.
eaten

Begira-begira jarrita, Pernandok esan zion ardiari:
Staring | putting | Pernando | said | did | to the sheep

—Ah txepela!... Bart harrapatu haun horrek
Ah | well done! | Yesterday night | caught | this | that
the one that caught this | that one

ez al zian kaikurik?
not | (question) | did have | any bucket

HARRIA ERREKARA

————

HARRIA ERREKARA
Stone   To The Stream

Beste batean Pernando, gauerdia ezkero eta izotz
Other   in a   Pernando   midnight   after   and   ice
  Another time   frost

gogorra   zen   gau   batean   etxera   etorri   zen.
 hard   it was night in one   home   come   did
 severe

Emazteak ez ordea aterik ireki nahi.
(His) wife not however door   open want

Arren egin zion,   atea   irekitzeko, baina alperrik.
Despite make did   the door   to open   but   in vain
  He pleaded with her

Oihuak esaten zion:
 Shouts   saying   to her-did
He shouted to her

—Zurekin gurutze donea hartutako senarrari aterik
 With you   cross   saintly   taken   husband   shelter
           on the holy cross

irekitzen **ez** **badiozu,** **nire** **burua** **errekara**
opening not if you don't my the head river
self

botatzera **noa.**
to throw I go

Hala **ere** **ez** **zen** **aterik** **irekitzen.**
That way also not did door opening

—Orduan **Pernandok** **soro-barrengo** **ormatik** **harri**
Then Pernando field-inner from the wall rock

handi **bat** **atera,** **eta** **hots** **handia** **eginez** **errekara**
big one remove and noise great making to the stream

bota **zuen.**
throw it-did

Emaztea **garrasika** **erdi-jantzian** **irten** **zen.**
The wife screaming half-dressed come out was

Pernandok **beste** **aldetik** **etxean** **sartu** **eta** **barrutik**
Pernando other side from home in entered and inside

atea **itxi** **zuen;** **eta** **bera** **bero-bero** **zegon**
the door close it-did and itself very hot was

bitartean,   emazte   gajoa   kanpoan,   hotzak   dar
as long as   wife   poor   outside   cold   shivering

dar   goiz   arte   eduki   zuen.
shivering   morning   until   keep   did

ILARGIRA ZENBAT BIDE?

ILARGIRA   ZENBAT   BIDE?
To The Moon   How Many   Roads
How many roads to the moon

Behin,   bidean   barrena   zetorrela,   bi   praile
Once   on the road   along   (he) was coming   two   friar
                                                         friars

aurkitu zituen.
  find   did
he met

—Pernando   —esan   zion   praile haietako batek, zuk
  Pernando   say   him-did   friar   from those   one   you
                    said   one of the friars

gizon   azkar,   buru argi,   bizkorren izena daramazu;
 man   quick   head   light   quickest   name   carry
                    bright mind   they say you're smart

eta esango   al   ginduzuke, hemendik   ilargira
and   will tell   (question)   would you   from here   to the moon

zenbatsu bide dagoen?
 how many   roads   there-are

Pernandok buruari hatz eginaz erantzuten dio:
Pernando | head-to | finger | doing | answering | says

—Galdera hori zail-xamarra dala deritzot.
Question | that | somewhat difficult | is | I think

—Baina zu azkarra zara-eta...
But | you | fast / clever | you are-also

—Hala ere: hemendik ilargirako hori oso zaila da.
That way / Even | also / so | from here | to the moon | that | very | difficult | is

Ilargitik honera balitz, zerbait esan nezake.
from the moon | here | if it were | something | say | (I) could

—Ea, bada, ilargitik onera zenbat bide
Let's see | so | from the moon | to here | how many | roads

dagon.
are there

—Zenbat bide dagon, ez dakit; bainan,
How many | roads | there are | not | (I) know | but

eguerdiko hamabiak laurden gutxitan
noon | twelve o'clock | quarters | shortly before
if just before twelve o'clock noon

ilargitik
from the moon

praile bat botako balute,
friar   one   throw   they would
they would throw a friar

eguerdiko hamabi-hamabietan
noon   twelve-thirty
at twelve-thirty noon

errektore etxean
(the) rector   home
at the parochial's home

bazkari-zain egongo litzake.
lunch-waiting   will be   could
waiting for lunch he would be

NON DEZU SEMEA?

NON DEZU SEMEA?
Where You Have Son
Where is your son?

Beste batean, semearekin zituen zer-asmatua.
Other one in with his son he had something-invented
Another time

Beretzako, bazkaria erretore-etxean bazuen.
For himself lunch in the rectory he had

Semearentzat ez ordea. Non bilatu semearentzat
For the son not however Where search for the son
to find

bazkaria?
lunch

Erretore-etxeko ateetara eraman zuen, eta, "nik
(The) rector's house to the doors brought him-did and I

deitu arte hago hemen", esanaz, bera jan-gelara
called until stay here saying, himself dining room
(imperative)

igo   zen.
went up   did

Bazkaltzen   hastekoan   Pernando   besteen   gain
Eating (lunch)   when starting   Pernando   of others   above

oihuka hasi zen:
screaming start did

—Aitaren... eta Espiritu Santuaren izenean.
Of the father and (the) Spirit   Holy   in the name

Erretoreak esaten dio orduan:
The rectors   say   him   time-on
                      then

—Pernando,   gaizki ari zera: Egizu   berriro
Pernando   wrong task that   Do   again
           you're doing it wrong   (imperative)

Aitaren.
(the) Father's (prayer)

Eta Pernandok berriz ere:
And   Pernando   again   also

—Aitaren... eta Espiritu Santuaren izenean.
Father's   and   Spirit   Holy   in the name of

Baina, Pernando, non duzu semea?
But · Pernando · where · you have · (the) son

—Ah! Beheran dago. Berehala etorriko da.
Ah · Down · is · Right away · will come · is
· · He's downstairs

Eta esan eta egin, ekarri eta berekin
And · to say · also · to do · bring · and · with him
Thus · said · thus · done · he brought him

bazkaritan jarri zuen.
for lunch · put · did
· sit down

EMAN BEHARKO

EMAN BEHARKO
Give   Have to
One Should Give

Amezketako   erretore-etxean   **apaiz batzuek**
(The) Amezketa of   rectory-in   priest   some
    In the rectory of Amesketako   some priests

bazkaria omen zuten,   eta,   bazkari usainera,
lunch   supposedly they did   and   lunch   smell-to
were having lunch one time   to the smell of the lunch

eguerdi   ingururako Pernando ere han   omen
noon   neighborhood-into Pernando   also there supposedly
at noon   in the neighborhood

zebilen.   Apaiz haiek   Pernando   bidali nahi
was wandering   Priest   they   Pernando   send   want
          Those priests   wanted to send

omen   zuten handik   patxarago bazkaltzeko,
supposedly   they did from there   quieter   to lunch
                  away   so they could lunch in peace

baina   ezin inola   ere.
but   couldn't no way   also
          in any way

Azkenik, bati hauxe bururatu omen zitzaion:
Finally   to one   this   occur   supposedly   did to him
(priest)

opoak atariko atean jarri eta kanpo-aldera nork
pumpkins   entrance at   door at   put   and   outside-towards   who

opo salto handiagoa egin. Pernandoren aldia
pumpkins   jump   larger   does   Pernando's   turn
      farther

zetorrenean, honek ere bere saltoa egingo zuen,
was coming   this   also   his   jump   will do   he-did

besteak bezala, kale aldera, eta orduan atea itxi
the others   like   street   towards   and   then   the door   close

eta kanpoan utziko zuten.
and   outside   leave   they did

Bai zera! Apaiz batek bere saltoa egin zuen.
Yes   that   Priest   a   his   jump   make   did
That's how it should go   A priest

Gero besteak. Besteak gero. Eta Pernandoren aldia
Then   others   Others   then   And   Pernando's   turn

iritsi zenean, opoak jarri zituen atariko atean...
arrive   did   pumpkins   put   did   entrance's   door at

baina bera barrura begira zela.
but   itself   inside   looking   was

—Nik, egingo deten pixka barren-aldera egingo dut
I   will do   they   (a) little   inward   will do   I
      what will I do

—esanez,   salto   egin   zuen,   eta
saying   jump   make   did   and

kanpora joan beharrean barrenerago sartu zen.
outside   go   instead of   further inside   entered   he did
     instead of outside,

4666666666
66666666

6

GATZAREN ARRAK

GATZAREN ARRAK
Salt's Effects

Sal erosketan ibiltzen ziran bi lagunek,
Salt shopping for walking they did two friends

Pernando zirikatu nahian esan zioten behin:
Pernando goad wanting to say they did once
wanting to goad Pernando they said to him

—Gaizki gabiltza, Pernando. Zu gizon azkarra zara
Bad we are Pernando You man fast are you
In trouble are a clever man

eta ia estutasun honetatik ateratzen gaituzun.
and already distress from this out you take us

—Zer da bada?
What is it then

—Bi itsasontzi bete gatz erosi ditugu, eta arrak
Two ships full (of) salt bought have and maggots

egin zaizkio   bidean.   Egin ahalak eginda ere,
do   is to it   on the way   Do   efforts done   even
formed on it (the salt)   Despite all efforts

ezin arrak   kendu dizkiogu...
can't maggots remove from them-we have
we could not remove the maggots from them

—Mandoaren esnea bota   iezaiozue, eta laster asko
   Mule's   milk   throw   you do to it   and   soon   much

joango zaizkio arrak   gatzari bai.
will go   is to it   maggots to the salt yes
will leave from it   from the salt

—Mando-esnea? Mandoak ez   du   esnerik   izaten,
   Mule's-milk   Mules   not   do   any milk   produce

gizona.
   man

—Ez eh?
 Not   hey

Ezta   gatzak   ere   arrak
Neither   salts   also   maggots
                  (produce)

Pernandoren bizkarretik
   Pernando's   from behind
   Pernando   trick

ez duzue egingo barrik.
not you will   will do   again

ODOLKIRIK BIDALTZEN AL DUZUTE?

ODOLKIRIK	BIDALTZEN	AL	DUZUTE?
Bloodletting	Sending	(question)	do
When killing a pig	send parts as gifts		you do?

Herri	txikietan,	norbaitek	txerria	hiltzeri	duanean,
Country	small towns	someone	pig	killing	when you do
			if someone kills a pig		

auzokoei	odolki	edo	txerri	puskaren	bat
neighbors	blood sausage	or	pig	part	one
to the neighbors					

bidaltzen	zaie.	Pernandok	ez	zuen,	ordea,
sending	are-to them	Pernando	not	did	however
	(zai-e)				

behin	ere	txerririk	hiltzen,	eta
once	also	pigs	kill	and

berari	bidalitako	erregaloak	ez	zuten	ordainik
to him	been sent	gifts	not	they did	payment-any
for the gifts sent to him			not ever	they had	repaid

izaten.	Aspertu	ziren	herrikoak	eman	eta	ez
have	Bored	did	townspeople	give	and	not
been	Tired	got	the townspeople	of to give		

hartzez, eta inork ez zion Pernandori
receiving and nobody not have-to him-did to Pernando
to receive (zi-o-n)

ezer bidaltzen.
anything sending

Hori ikusi zuenean, txerria hiltzea gogoratu
That to see when he did pig killing remember

zitzaion Pernandori. Hil zuen eta odolki eta
did to him to Pernando Kill he did it and blood sausage and

gaineratikoak ontzi batean harturik, hasi zen
the rest container in one having taken start did
went

aterik ate.
door to door

—Gure etxera odolkirik bidaltzen al duzue zuek?
Our home bloodletting sending (question) you will you
Are you going to send us bloodletting gifts?

—Ez...
No

—Orduan hemen ez daukat zorrik —esanaz,
Then here not I have debt by saying

ezer   utzi gabe   aurrera joaten zen.
anything   left   without   forward   to go   did
without leaving anything he continued

Amezketarrak,   Pernando   ere
By those of Amezketa   Pernando   also
  The Amezketarrians

txerria hiltzen   hasi   zsela   ikusi   zutenean,
  pig   kill   to start   was   see   when they did
     started killing pigs   when they saw

   berriz   hasi   ziren   bere   etxera   odolkiak
on the other hand   start   they did   his   home-to   blood sausages

bidaltzen.
  sending
to send

Pernandok, ordea, bere bizi guztian ez zuen berriz
Pernando   however   his   life   entire   not   did   again

txerririk hil.
  a pig   kill

ELKAR HIL

ELKAR   **HIL**
Each other   Kill

Aurretik	**ibiltzen**	**zen**	**ardi**	**eskurakoi,**	**maite**	**bat**
Since before	walking	did	sheep	close at hand	beloved	one
	it used to walk			tame		one favorite

zuen	**Pernandok.**		**Elkar**	**esaten**	**zioten**
to him-did	Pernando		Each other	saying	they did
	Pernando had			They called "Each other"	

ardi   **horri.**
sheep   that
that sheep

Behin	**batean**		**Elkar**	**gaixotu**	**zitzaion,**		**eta**
Once	in a		Each other	ill	did to him		and
Once upon a time			(that sheep)	fell ill			

abel	**sendalariari**		**deitu**		**arren,**
cattle	healer-to		called		despite
	for a vet				

ez	**zen**	**agiri**	**eta**	**ez**	**zen**	**agiri.**	**Ardia**	**hil**	**zen,**
not	did	appear	and	not	did	appear	(The) sheep	die	did
		didn't come at all							

eta barruak saski batean hartuta han joan ziren
and his inside basket in a having taken there go did
    its innards   in a basket

Pernando eta bere emaztea errekan garbitzera.
Pernando and his wife in the stream to clean

Irtetzerakoan,   Pernandok
  When leaving   Pernando

esan zion etxean gelditu zen semeari:
say did home stop did to (his) son
         at home stopping, said

—Gure galdezka inor etortzen baldin baduk,
  Our asking nobody come if if you do

  Elkar hilda errekan gaudela esan hiok.
Each other killing in the stream we are say that
(the sheep)

Laster etorri zen abel sendalaria. Zaldi eta guzti
  Soon come did cattle healer Horse and all

atarira sartu zen, eta sukaldeko atetik burua
  hall entered did and (the) kitchen of door-from head

sartuaz:
  sticking

—Eup!... —esan zuen—. Ama eta aita non dira,
Hey! say did Mother and father where are

txikito?
little one

—Elkar hilda errekan daude...
Each other killing in the stream they are

Abel sendalaria, hori entzun bezain agudo, joan
(The) cattle healer that heard as quickly went
hearing that

zen sendalariaren etxera, eta erretorearen etxera,
did (the) healer's home and (the) rector's home
the priest's

eta han eraman zituen errekara guztiak
and there bring did to the stream all

arrapastaka. Han ez zeudela ikusi zutenean,
hurriedly There not there were-that see when they did

Pernandoren etxera joan ziran egin ahalak
Pernando's home go they did (emphasis) efforts

eginez, senar-emazteak elkar hilda arkituko
making husband-wife each other dead find

zituztelakoan,   baina...   bai   zera!...   ondo   patxaran
expecting   but   yes   that   well   calmly

zeuden   biak   sukaldean   Elkar   goxoaren   gibela
were   both   in the kitchen   Each other's (the sheep's)   delightful   liver

jaten.
eating

ASTOA ETA ESKRIBAUA

ASTOA · ETA · ESKRIBAUA
(The) Donkey · And · (The) Scribe

Alegiko · eskribauarentzat, Pernando · zirikatzea
From Alegia · for the scribe · Pernando · teasing
For the scribe from Alegia, teasing Pernando

bezalako · festarik · ez · zen.
like · no holiday · not · did
was as if there was no holiday

Behin · hasi · zen · beti · bezala · ziri · eta · ziri,
Once · start · did · always · as · barbing · and · barbing
Once started · as usual · teasing · teasing

artzainak · ezer · ez · zekitela · esaten.
sheep-person-the · anything · not · knew · saying
that the shepherd · nothing

—Ezetz? · —esan · zion · Pernandok—. Eskribauak
No? · say · to him-did · Pernando · Scribes

gutxiago. · Nire · astoak · ulertzen
less · My · donkey · understanding
language

duena   ezetz berorrek paperean jarri?
does-the one   not   you (formal)   on paper   put
        you haven't

—Jarriko ez dut, bada, gizona?
  Put   not have   so   man
                      what if

—Ia... ia... Jarri beza arre!
Ee-aa ee-aa   Put   let   go
               Put it there then?

—Jarria dago.
 Placed   is
It's put (on paper)

—Jarri beza...   isooo!...
 Put   let   eeeesoooo
Now put this (on paper)

Jarria dago.
Placed   is

—Orain   jarri beza   hau...   —Eta   mingaina
 Now   put   let   this   And   tongue
           let's put   this on paper

   aho-sapaian   jarriaz
   mouth-roof on   positioning
on the roof of the mouth   clicking

   astoari   arinago ibili dadin egiten   zaion
at the donkey   faster   walk   may   doing   to it-is made
              to make the donkey walk faster

hotsa egin zion.
noise (emphasis) to him-did
that noise made for him

—Hori paperean jarriko duenik ez da oraindik jaio
That on paper put-will who not is still born
           will put   is not born yet

—esan zuen eskribauak.
say to him-did (the) scribes
   said to him

—Hori nire astoak ederki daki bada... Astoa,
That my donkey great knows so Donkey

eskribaua baino gehiago, arranotan!
(a) scribe than more hell!
   better than a scribe (exclamation)

69

HARRI, ASTOA...

HARRI, ASTOA...
Stone   Donkey

Behin batean, bazihoan Pernando   feriatik   etxera,
Once   in a   was going   Pernando   from the fair   to home
Once upon a time

bere astotxoaren atzetik.
his   little donkey   behind

Bidean   topo   egin,   zuan   azkar   usteko
On the way   encounter   (emphasis)   to him-did   quick   presumably

batekin, eta hona nola hitz   egin   zuten
with one   and   here   how   word   (emphasis)   they did
                                              chat

—Nondik   zatoz,   Pernando?
From where   come   Pernando
                did you come

—Feriatik.
From the fair.

—Laboreak   zer   egin du?
Crops   what   do   does
             which onesyou do

—Zai eta irin, zai eta irin.
Wheat and flour wheat and flour

—Hori   ez   dizut   galdetzen,   Plazako
That   not   (I) will to you   ask   (with) the square's

gora-behera galdetzen dizut:
ups-and-downs   ask   to you (I) will

—Zaldian gorago, asto   txikian baino.
On horse higher donkey small-in than
                   or rather on a small donkey

—Zer   asto   eta   asto-ondo!...
What   donkey   and   donkey-like

Zure horrek kargak aurreregi dauzka behintzat.
Your   that   loads   too soon   has   at least
Your donkey seems to be carrying too much

—Ordubeteko bidean   aurrerago baleuzka nahiko
One-hour   on the way further ahead if they had sufficient

nuke.
(I) would

71

Harri astoa, harri,
Stone donkey stone

iluntzerako ote gaitezkeen
by evening maybe could

atarian jarri,
at the door put

ezer irabazten ez dugu eta
anything winning not is and
      earning   (lit. we have)

mintzatu arren gizon horri.
speak despite man that

PLAST!

PLAST!
Splash

Gure Pernando bazihoan bada behin festara, eta,
Our   Pernando   was going   so   once   to the party   and

bidean, ibai-ertzean, gizon bat ikusi zuen.
on the way on the riverbank   man   one   see   he-did

—Zertan zaude hor, gizona? —galdetu zion
In what   you are   there   man   ask   him-did

Pernandok.
Pernando

—Hara bada: ibaiaren beste aldera joan nahi nuke,
To there then   river's   other   side to   go   want   (I) would

eta ez nuke busti nahi eta...
and not (I) would get wet want   and

—Ez estutu, gizona; neronek bizkarrean eramango
Not tighten man I myself on (my) back will carry
stress

zaitut. Igo...
you Climb up

Jarri zitzaion gizon hori bizkar gainean, eta
Set did to him man that (his) back on top and

ibaiaren erdi-aldera iristean hala dio
river's mid-river upon arriving that way says
thus

goikoak:
the above
the guy on top

Pernando, Amezketako bertsolaria:
Pernando (the from) Amezketa bard

ez zihoak hire gainean gaizki
not go yours on top wrong
it suits you well

Errezilgo zapateria.
Errezil from shoe store
(like) from the Errezil shoe store

Eta Pernandok, azpitik gora begiratuaz, erantzun
And Pernando under up looking up answered

zion:
did

Hirekin badakarrek nahiko janaria,
With you   bring   sufficient   food

laster izango duk nahiko edaria.
soon   have   you do sufficient   drink

Eta plast!, errekara bota zuen.
And splash to the stream throw did

BOST UME, LAU TITI

BOST UME, LAU TITI
Five   Calf   Four   Tit
          Calves   Tits

Buru-hausterik handienak Pernandori
Head-breaking   (the) biggest   to Pernando
      Pernando's biggest headache or worry

sabela   betetzeak eman zizkion.
(the) stomach   filling   give   he owed
was filling his stomach

Eskerrak sabel   bat besterik ez zuela.   **Arako**
Thanks   stomach one   else   not having   Of Ara
      Thankfully he had only one stomach

Santu arrek nahi zuela esan oi   duten   bezela,
Saint   males   want   had   say   oi   they have-that   like
  (the) saints   as they supposedly had said   if only they had

bi sabel izan balitu,   **istilu gorriak**
two   bellies (past)   had   uproar   red
      had two bellies   great trouble

ikusi beharrean izango zan.
see   instead of   will be   was
(he) would see instead

Batek ere lana nahikoa eman zion.
One also work enough give to him-did
Even one gave to him

Entzun bestela gertaera au.
Listen otherwise event this
Just listen to this story

Tolosako herrian zan, lau gizon ari ziran
Tolosa in the village was four man working they did
In the village of Tolosa

alaitasun pozgarrian zaunk eta zurrut egiten. Aien
joy happily yap and drink doing Oh my
yapping and drinking

jateko ekiñaldia! Inguruari begiratu gabe ere
to eat effort surroundings look without also
and eat they did it even looked like

plateretik albora jakiak airean zebiltzan.
from the plate aside foods in the air were floating
food was being thrown around

Pernando alderatu zitzaien eta berari begira
Pernando appeared he did to them and to him looking
to it

irrikitzen zegon.
eagerly was

Ez ordea inork jaramonik egiten. Begira egotez
Not however nobody attention doing Looking being

aspertu zan, eta ala dio gure Pernandok:
bored was and thus says our Pernando
tired

—Gure herrian ere komeri ederra gertatu da.
Our village in also amusing incident beautiful happened is

—Zer ba? Zer ba? —galdetu zioten bestia, jatez
What well What well ask they did others eating

ia geldituan.
almost stopped

—Behi batek bost ume egiten ditu.
Cow one five calves doing has
got

—Gizona, gizona —zioten besteek— behi harrek
Man man they did the others cow that

zenbat titi ditu ba?
how many udder has well

—Zenbat izango ditu? Lau.
How many have has Four

—Eta bostgarrenak zer egiten du?
And fifth what doing does

—Zer egingo du! Nik orain egiten dutena
What will do does I now doing what I am doing

bera. Besteei begira egon.
itself to others looking stay
the same   am

Ori entzun zutenean berarekin jaten jarri erazi
That hear when they did with them eating put made

zuten, eta bostetan kamutsena ez zela Pernandok
they did and five of humblest not was Pernando
             from the five the humblest   he was

erakutsi zuen.
show did
showed

OINETAKOAK MERKE

————

OINETAKOAK MERKE
   SHOES   CHEAP

Bataioren batera joateko,   edo   ezteietara joateko,
Baptism   together   to go   or   weddings   to go
  For to go to a baptism   to go to a wedding

edo   alkate egin   zutelako,   edo
 or   mayor (emphasis) because they made   or
     or because they made him mayor

zertarako, edo zergatik ez dakigu, baina Pernandok
what for   or   why   not   know   but   Pernando
  or for whatever reason we don't know

oinetako berri batzuk behar   omen   zituen. Baino...
footwear   new   some   need apparently he had   But
 new shoes   apparently needed

betikoa!, dirurik   ez.
the usual any money not
  he had no money

Hala   ere, joan zen oinetakogile batengana.
That way also went   did   shoemaker   one-to

—Oinetako horiek zenbatekoak dira?
Footwear   those   how much   are
  Shoes

—Horiek? —esan zion saltzaileak barre egiteagatik—.
Those   say   did   salesperson   laugh   for doing
                                          laughing

Ezkerreko oinekoa hutsean, eta eskuinekoa hogei
(The) left   foot   empty   and   right one   twenty
                   free

peseta.
peseta

—Eta beste pare hau?
And   other   couple   this

—Hau hogei peseta (ezkerreko oinekoa erakutsiaz),
This   twenty   peseta   left   footwear   showing

eta eskuinekoa hutsean.
and   right one   empty
                 free

—Orduan bada... hau eta hauxe eramango ditut
Then   so   this   and   this   will take   have

—erantzun zuen Pernandok oinetako pare
answered   did   Pernando   footwear   couple

bakoitzetik hutsean zena hartuaz.
from each · empty · that was · taking
· the free

Jarri zituen biak eta hasi zen korrika. Bai
Put · did · both · and · started · did · running · Yes

saltzailea ere atzetik "horri... horri... lapurra..."
seller · also · behind · to that · to that · thief
· · catch him · catch him

deiadarka.
shouting

Halakoren batean norbaitek heldu zion besotik,
Such-of · in one · someone · grab · to him-did · by the arm
At one instance · · grabbed him

baina Pernandok, sua zeriola, esan zion:
but · Pernando · fire · burning · say · did to thim

—Hago geldi, kankailu ori,
Be · still · big guy · that
Leave it · that big guy

korrika apustua diagu eta.
running · bet · we have · so
we are racing together

Eta berriz han joan zen arin asko, oinetako
And · again · there · go · did · quickly · much · (the) footwear

saltzailea   atzean   utzita.
salesperson   behind   leaving

MAS CARGA

MAS   CARGA
MORE   LOAD

Gerratean,   Pernandok   Betelura   bagajea   eraman
In war   Pernando   to the front   luggage   brought

behar   zuen.   Hartu   zituen   hiru   mando,   eta
have to   he-did   Take   did   three   mule(s)   and
                   He took

soldaduak   hasi   ziren   mando   gainean   zama   jartzen.
the soldiers   start   did   mule   over   load   putting

Jarri   eta   jarri,   mandoak   lehertzeko   zorian   zeuden,
Put   and   put   mules   to collapse   about to   were

eta   hala   ere,   soldaduak   ez   zioten   zama   jartzeari
and   that way   also   the soldiers   not   they did   load   placing
                                                                 with loading

uzten.
 leave
stop

Nahikoa zela esan nahi zien   Pernandok;   baina
Enough   was   say   want did to them   Pernando   but
Wanted to say that it was enough to them,

erdaraz jakin ez, eta   ezin   esan.
in Spanish know not and couldn't say

Hala,   zapatariari galdetu omen   zion   ia
That way to the shoemaker asked   apparently him-did almost

nahikoa   zela   nola   esaten   zen   erdaraz,   eta
enough   was   how   saying   was   in Spanish   and

zapatariak esan zion "más carga" (jarri gehiago)
shoemakers   say   did   more   load   put   more

esaten zela.
saying   was

Soldaduak   zenbat   eta zama gehiago jarri, orduan
The soldier   how many and   load   more   put   then

eta haserreago Pernandok esaten zuen "más carga,
and   angrier   Pernando   saying he-did more   load

más   carga...". Mandoak   lurra   jotzeko zeudenean,
more   load   Mules   the earth to beat   were

Pernandok   mandoan   gaineko   zama   guztia
Pernando   on the mule   over   load   everything

   lurrera   botaz, esan   omen   zuen:
to the ground   throwing   say   apparently   he-did

Más   carga,   más   carga
More   load   more   load

hiru   mando   eta   bost   karga?
three   mule   and   five   load

Hartutako   lekuan
   Taken   the place-in

bertan   deskarga.
   there   download

Herri   honetan   zapatari
Village   this   shoemaker

presturik   ez   al   da?
   ready   not   (question)   is
(ready to take the mule's place)

HILDA APOSTUA IRABAZI

HILDA APOSTUA IRABAZI
(A) Dead   (A) Bet   Won

Pernandok talkarako   ahari   bat   omen   zeuken:
Pernando   for bumping   ram   one   supposedly   he had
            a headbutting male sheep

eta beti erronkan hemen   zebilen,   beste nonbait
and always challenge-in here   he was being other anywhere

harekin   jokatzeko   haina   zen   aharirik   bazen,
with that   to play for   enough   did   enough   there was

Amezketako   plazara ekarri zezatela esanaz.
(the) Amezketako square-to bring   they had   saying

Halako batean, izugarrizko ahari handi bat ekarri
Such   in a   scary   ram   big   one bring
At one instance

omen   zioten Azkoititik.
supposedly they did from Azkoitia

—Ia   Pernando —esan zioten—. Hire ahariari honek
Almost   Pernando   say   they did   Your   ram-to   this
Let's see

jokatuko ziok...
to play-will   to you-will

—Bai, nahi badik. Baina garbi jokatu behar diagu.
Yes   want   has   But   clean   to play   must   we have
             if is

Hara hemen arrasto bat (eginrz)... hara   hemen
There   here   trace   one   done   to there   here

bestea...   Horien barruan jokatzera,   eta
the other   Those-of   inside   to play   and
              Inside of those (traces) they'll play

arrasto horien   artetik   azken   irteten
trace   those-of   among   last-in   coming out
  of the traces   from between   the last to come out

denak irabaztea. Konforme   al   gara?
all   winning   Agreed   (question) we are?
   is the winner

—Jakina bada!...
Of course   so

Hau   entzutean Pernando joan zen ikuilura, eta
This   hearing   Pernando   go   did   stable-to   and

ilunpean,   giltzapean,   inori   erakutsi   gabe
darkness-in   under lock   to anyone   show   without
                 without showing anyone

edukitzen   zuan   ahari   zahar,   elbarritu,   txutik
holding   to him-did   ram   old   crippled   motionless
     he kept an old ram

ezin   egon   zen   bat   sokatik   zuela   agertu   zen.
couldn't   stay   was   one   from the rope   having   appear   did

A   zer   parrak   egin   zituzten   azkoitarrek
Ah   what   laughs   (emphasis)   they had   the Azkois

ahari   zahar   hura   ikustean!
ram   old   that   upon seeing
seeing that old ram

Esanak   esan,   aurrez   aurre   jarri   zituzten   bi
Tales   say   before   face   put   they did   (the) two

ahariak   talka   egin   zezaten.   Lehenengo
rams   collision   (emphasis)   they wanted   The first in

erasoan,   Azkoitiko   ari   bikainak   jo   zuen
attack   the one from Azkoita   being   excellent   hit   he-did

indarrez   Pernandorena,   eta   han   utzi   zuen   lepoa
with strength   the one of Pernando   and   there   left   he-did   neck

hausita, bertan hilda. Beste aharia hilda zegoela
exhausted there dead Other sheep dead was

ikustean, azkoitiarra irten zen arrasto artetik...
upon seeing those from Azkois come out did trace among

eta bai apustua galdu ere. Pernandorena
and yes bet lost also The one from Pernando

irten zen azken!
come out did (in) last

TONTO AZKARRA

TONTO   AZKARRA
Foolish   Fast
            Clever

Pernando   eta   bere   emaztea   ari   ziren   behin
Pernando   and   his   wife   being did   once

mendian,   bere   gurdia   garoz   betetzen.
the mountain-in his   cart   with ferns filling

Hala   ari   zirela,   zauritutako   erbi   bat   etorri
Thus   being they were wounded   hare   one   came

zitzaien   ingurura;   hartu   eta   garo   artean
he did to them around   took   and   the ferns between

ezkutatu   zuten.   Handik   pixka batera,
hide   they did   From there little together
                                Shortly after

erbi-zakurrak   etorri   ziren   usainean,   eta
beagles   come   were   smelling   and

gurdi-ingurutik   ezin   kendu zituzten. Ehiztariak
wagon-wheel-from   couldn't   remove   they did   Hunters

etorri ziren hurrena.
come   were   next

—Erbirik ikusi   al   duzue? —galdetu   zien
Any hares   saw   (question) you have?   ask   did to them

senar   emazteei   ehiztarietako batek.   Eta,
husband (and) wife-to   of the hunters   one   And
to the husband and wife   one of the hunters

Pernandok erantzun zion:
Pernando   answer   him-did

—Orain   hamaikak   inguru.
(It's) now   eleven (o'clock)   around

Ehiztariak berriro:
Hunters   again

—Erbirik ikusi duzuen?
Any hares   saw   you have?

Pernandok:
Pernando

—Oraindik behintzat gehienaz ere hamaika eta
Still / at least / at most / also / eleven / and

erdiak.
halves
a half

Eta "tontoa duk gizon hau" esanda,
And / "the dumb one" / you do / man / this / having said
this man is a fool

urrutiratu ziren ehiztariak.
moved away / they did / (the) hunters

Hurrengo larunbatean Tolosan ikusi zuten
Next / Saturday / Tolosan / saw / they did

Pernando ehiztariak. Eta zirikatzeagatik galdetu
Pernando / hunters / And / for teasing / asked

zioten:
they did

—Hi, tonto, zer ordu duk?
Hey! / fool / what / time / you do

Eta Pernandok erantzun zien:
And / Pernando / answered / did to them

—Ederra zegoen. Andreak eta biok   jan genuen.

Beautiful   it was   The wife   and   we two   eat   we did

My wife and I ate it

Ehiztariak harrituta gelditu ziren.

Hunters   surprised   stop   did

—Arranoa!

Eagle

Ederrak eman zizkiguk!

Beautiful   give   to us-gave

It gave us something great

Ez zegok hori tonto txarra!...

Not there is that fool   bad

That fool wasn't so bad

ASTOA POZEZ SALTOKA

ASTOA POZEZ SALTOKA
Donkey   Happy   Jumping

Atxo   gaixoa!   Egin   ahalak eginda ere,
Poor   sick one   (emphasis) efforts   done   also
                                   Whatever efforts were made

ezin astoa mugitu. "Arre   eta   arre",   astoa
couldn't donkey Translating...   Go   and   go   donkey
      donkey couldn't move

atzera. Egundaino horrelakorik!...
back   Until now   (not) anything like that

—Zer du   asto horrek, amonatxo? —galdetu zion
What   does donkey   that   grandma   asked   did

Pernandok.
Pernando

—Ez dakigu bada. Ez ibili nahi.
Not   know   so   Not walk wants

—Jakin egin behar, jakin...
Know (emphasis) have to know

—Jakin? Ia bada zuk aurrera joan erazten
Know Almost so you forward went allowing

duzun.
you have

—Baita pozez saltoka jarri ere.
Also happy jumping put also

—Ia, ia zure "abilidade" ori.
Almost almost your skill that

Pernandok ezkutura joan eta ardagai puska bat
Pernando left went and kindling piece one

piztu zuan. Gero, astoaren aldamenera etorri,
lit to him-did Then donkey's to the side of came

eta belarri batetik hitz egingo balio bezala jarri
and ear from one word will do value like put
courage

zen, eta bitartean beste belarri-zulotik ardagai
did and while other ear-hole burning straw

piztua **sartu** **zion.** **Astoa** **laster** **hasi** **zen** **ipur**
lit entered did Donkey soon start it was tail

saltoka, **gainean** **zeramazkian** **ontzi** **guztiak**
jumping over was carrying container all

hausteko **zorian.**
to break about to

Atsotxoak, **harrituta,** **beldurtuta,** **galdetu** **zion**
The old woman surprised frightened asked did

Pernandori:
to Pernando

—**Baina** **zer** **esan** **diozu?**
But what word you say

—**Ah!...** **Ipuin** **politak...**
Ah Story nice

—**Zer** **esan** **diozu** **horrela** **aztoratzeko?**
What word you way like that to upset
to make it move

—**Zer?** **Garagar,** **olo** **eta** **arto** **asko** **dagoela** **aurten,**
What Barley millet and corn many is-that this year

eta etxera joandakoan, guztietatik nahi adina
and home when returning from all want as many

emango diozula.
will give you say

ATOZ BAZKALTZERA...

ATOZ BAZKALTZERA...
Come   To Lunch

Herri koxkor batean zan.
Town   small   in one   was
    It was in a small town

Eguerdiko orduak aurrera zihoazen.   Pernandoren
Of noon   hours   forward   went   Pernando's
    The noon hours were passing by

bazkaltzeko   gogoak   aurrerago   oraindik,   baina
  to lunch   desires   further ahead   still   but

  inondik   ere   sabela   betetzeko biderik   ez
by any means   also   (the) stomach   to fill   way   not

zuen ikusten.
he did   see

Hontan,   apaiz jaun bat agertu   zen. Pernando
At that moment   priest   man   one   appear   did   Pernando
           a priest

alderatu zitzaion eta agur itzaltsu bat eginez esan
approach   he did   and   hello   somber   one   making   say
a sad greeting

zion:
him-did

—**Jauna: galdera bat, barkatu behar dit.**
  Sir   question   one   forgive   must   to me
    one question   you must forgive me

—**Nahi duzun guztia.**
Desire   you have   everything
Anything you want

—**Horra ba, nik jakin nahi nukeena da... alegia...**
There   well   I   know   want   would like   is   that is to say
     would like to know

zera... Herri ontan bazkarietara norbait eraman
that   Town   in this   to meals   someone   bring
      to lunch invite someone

nahi denean, nola esaten zaio?
desire   is-when   how   saying   is
   you want   do you say that

—**Hori, era askotara.**
  That   kind   many
For that   there are many ways

—**Bai baina bat, esan bezait bat.**
  Yes   but   one   tell   let me   one

101

—Nola esango dizut bat... "Nirekin bazkarietara
How will tell (I) will to you one With me to meal
for lunch

etorri nahi bazenu,
come want if
if you want to come

poz handi bat emango zenidake".
joy big one will give you would give
you'd give me great joy

—Poz hori emango diot ba.
Joy that will give will give well

—Eh! Zer!
Hey What

—Berorrekin bazkarietara joango naiz.
With you for lunch will go I am

—Baina...
But

—Aspaldian, norbaitek horrelako zerbait
Long ago someone like that something
For a long time

esango ote zidan, zain nengoen.
will say maybe from me did waiting I was
would say to me

Eta nahi bazuen, eta nahi ez bazuen,
And desire he had and desire not he had
And whether he wanted or not

apaiz jaunak bazkarietara eraman behar izan
priest gentlemen for lunch bring must be
the priest

zuen.
he did

DUM... DAM... DUM... DAM...

DUM...   DAM...   DUM...   DAM...
Ding   Dong   Ding   Dong

Gau   batean,   etxera   joan   zenean,   bere   emaztea
Night in one   home   go   when he was   his   wife

haserre   eta   haurrak   gosez   negarrez   eta
angry   and   children   hungry   crying   and

zer   jantzirik   ez   zutela   aurkitu   zituan
what   wearing   not   them having   find   he was
anything to wear

Pernandok.
Pernando

Haiek   hala   ikusi   zituenean,   atera   zen   etxetik,
Them   that way   see   when he was   leave   did   from home

joan   zen   korrika   elizara,   igo   zen
go   did   running   to the church   went up   did

kanpandorrera eta hasi zen dum... dam... dum...
to the bell tower   and   started   did   ding   dong   ding

dam... hil-kanpaia indarrez jotzen.
dong   death-bell   with strength   hit

—Zein hil da, zein hil da, zein hil da?...
Who   killed   is   who   killed   is   who   killed   is

—galdetzen zuten amezketarrak estutasunez
ask   they did   by those of Amezketa   anxiousness

beterik. Inork ez zekien ezer.
full of   Nobody   not   knew   anything

Eliz aldera inguratu zirenean, Pernandoz esan
Church   towards   got close   when they did   to Pernando   say

zien kanpandorretik garrasika:
did to them   from the bell tower   yelling

—Herrian den beharrena hil da.
In the village   all   in need   killed   is

—Zein da, bada, zein?...
Who   is   so   who

Jo zuen kanpaia beste puska batean, eta berriz
Hit did bell other piece in one and again

ere:
also

—Herrian den beharrena hil da...
In the village all in need killed is

—Zein da, ordea gizona?
Who is however man

—Karitatea hil da. Horixe zen hemen beharrena!
Charity killed is Exactly it was here needed

Egia jakin zutenean, esan zioten Pernandori:
Truth know when they did say they did to Pernando

—Ez estutu, gizona. Zure emazte eta haurrekin
Not press man Your wife and children with
worry

hator bihar plazara, eta zerbait bilduko dugu
come tomorrow square-to and something gather we have
we will

zuentzat.
for you

Hurrengo goizean han agertu zen plazan, haur
Next morning in there appeared did square child

guztiak larrugorrian gurdian hartuta. Jantzi
all naked cart in having taken Dress

zituzten, eta hilabeterako zer jana eman ere bai.
they did and for a month what food give also yes

Egun hartan pozik joan zen Pernando.
Day in that happy go was Pernando

DON JUAN DE GARAIOA?

DON JUAN DE GARAIOA?
Don Juan Of Garaioa

Izurrite batean,   **mando gainean**   **gaixoak**
Epidemic   in one   (the) mule   onto   sick people
During an epidemic   on the mule

eramaten hasi zen   **Pernando.**   **Bakoitzarengatik**
carry   start   he did   Pernando   For each
    started to carry

hainbesteko bat ematen zioten, eta, kaixo mutil!
so much   one   give   they did   and   hello   boy
some amount

bapo zebilen.
very well   he was
he was doing very well

Tolosatik Hernanira gaixo bat eramateko agindu
From Tolosa   Hernani to   sick   one   to transport   ordered
     a patient

zioten behin. Bai berak agindua bete ere. Baina,
they did   once   Yes   she   the order   full (of)   also   But

Hernanira iritsi   zirenean,   gaixoak esan zion:
Hernani to   arrived when they did (the) patient say to him did

—Donostiraino joan nahi   nuke.   Eraman nazazu,
To Donostia   go   want   (I) would Take   me you

gizontxo.
little man

Hernanitik   Donostiraino   gaixo   ura   eramanda,
From Hernani   to Donostia   (the) patient water   carrying

Pernandok ez zuen   ezer   irabazten, eta ez zuela
Pernando   not did   anything   winning   and not having
                                   gaining

eramango esan zion.
will carry   say   him did

—Hernaniraino   ekartzeko   esan   didate   niri,   eta
Hernani to   to bring   say   they have to me   and

hemen gelditu beharko duzu.
here   stop   forcibly   you do
                     you have to

—Baina gizona...
But   man

—Esana   esanda   dago, eta kito.
Said   having said   is   and that's it

—Zer kito eta kito ondo! Kontu gero zer esaten
What do and do   well Care then what saying

duzun! Don Juan de Garaioa naiz gero ni...
you have Don Juan of Garaioa am   then me
                                 I am

—Bai eh?
Yes hey

Don Juan de Garaioa?
Don Juan of   Garaioa

Berdin da baldin bada
Equal   is   if   so

Infernuko arraioa.
Hell's   devil

Indarrez ez baldin bada
By force not   if   so

ni baino gehiago,
me than   more
(if you are) more than me

Pernando mandoarekin
Pernando   with the mule

etxera doa.
home   goes

BABAK ETA ARRAUTZAK

BABAK ETA ARRAUTZAK
Beans · And · Eggs

Amezketako mutil batek, nahi haina arrautza
(An) Amezketa · boy · one · wants · so much · egg

frijitu jateko gutizia izan zuan behin. Bai jan
fried · to eat · craving · (past) · to him-did · once · Yes · eat

ere. Ostatura joan eta zortzi sartu zituan tripatzar
also · (An) inn to · went · and · eight · entered · was · belly

hartan. Ordaindu ordea bat ere ez: ordainduko
in that · Pay · however · one · also · not · Pay for

zituela eta ordainduko zituela... baina ordaindu
having them · and · pay for · having them · but · pay

gabe Ameriketara joan zen.
without · America to · went · he did

Ameriketan hamar urte igaro, eta aberastuta etorri
In America / ten / years / spent / and / enriched / came

zen. Bere zorrak kilisk-kilisk egiten zion
he did / His / debts / fluttering / doing / to him did

bihotzean, eta ordaindu behar zuela eta, joan zen
in the heart / and / pay / must / having / and / go / he did

ostatu etxera.
(to the) inn / (at) home

—Hara bada —esan zion ostalariak— zortzi
To there / so / say / him-did / (the) innkeepers / eight

arrautza haietatik zortzi txita txiki atera
egg / from those / eight / chicks / small / take out

zitezkeen; zortzi txita haiek zortzi oilo izango
could be / eight / chicks / they / eight / chickens / have

ziren laster; zortzi oilo horiek urtean zortziehun
did / soon / eight / hens / those / a year / eight hundred

arrautza ipiniko zizkidaten; zortziehun arrautza...
egg / will lay / would give me / eight hundred / egg

hamar urte... bi mila oilo... hamasei mila
ten years two thousand hens small word

txita... hamabost mila peseta hortxe nonbait
thousand fifteen thousand peseta right there apparently

ibiliko dira.
be are

Mutila izutu zen. Baietz eta ezetz luzaroan
The boy frightened he did Yes and not for long

aditu eta gero, bakoitzak bere aldetik gizon bat
heard and then each his side from man one

jarri, bien artean hirugarren bat izendatu, eta
put between between the third one appoint and

haiek esaten zutena egitea erabaki zuten.
they saying what they were to do decided they did

Ostalariak lege-gizon ospetsu bat jarri zuen;
Innkeepers lawyer famous one put did

mutilak berriz Pernando. Elkarrekin hitz egiteko
the boy meanwhile Pernando Together word to do

egun eta ordua ipini zituzten: lege-gizona joan zen,
day and time put they did lawyer go did

baina gure Pernando ez zen agiri.
but our Pernando not did appear

Halako batean, han dator lasterka, izerdi
Such in one there (he) comes running sweat
In that instance

patsetan. Epaikariak, juezak, ala ikustean, esan
streaming When judges or upon seeing say

zion:
to him did

—Baina gizona, zuk
But man you

lehengo lepotik orain ere burua. Erlojua gelditu
earlier from the neck now also head Watch stop
haven't changed

egin al zaizu?
(emphasis) (question) to you-has

—Ez jauna, ez. Nere Mari-Joxepak atzo egositako
No sir no My Mari-Joxep yesterday cooked

babak   zeuzkan   lapikoan,   eta   haiexek   baratzean
beans   had-that   in the pot   and   those   in the garden

aldatzen   aritu   naiz.
changing   be   will
to plant

—A   gizarajo,   gizarajo,   gizarajoa!...   Egositako   babak
Ah   poor man   poor man   Damn!   Cooked   beans

hazitarako   ez   dituk   gauza,   gizona.
for digestion   not   you will   thing   man

—Ez   eh?   Ezta   orain   hamar   urte   jandako   arrautzak
Not   hey   Neither   now   ten   years   eaten   eggs

ere,   txitak   ateratzeko.
also   chicks   to get out

ARKUMEA ETA DUROA

ARKUMEA ETA DUROA
Lamb · And · Duro (coin)

Ez · dakigu · zertarako · baino, · behin, · besteren
Not · (we) know · what for · however · once · some

bordatik · arkume · bat · atera · nahian · zebilen
(sheep's) pen · (a) lamb · one · take out · wanting to · he was

Pernando. · Kanpo · aldetik · barrura · eskua · sartuta,
Pernando · Outside · side from · inside · the hand · inserted

isatsetik · heltzen · zion · arkumeari · eta
from the tail · holding · to him-did · (the) lamb to · and

langa-sareraino · ekarri · ere · bai, · baino · tarte · estuduna
to the gate-bars · bring · also · yes · than · gap · narrow

zen · langa · hori · eta · ezin · atera · zuen · arkumea
did · gate · that · and · couldn't · take out · he did · (the) lamb

kanpora. Bertan utzi behar izan zuen.
outside　　There　left　have to　(past)　he did
　　　　　He had to leave it there

Urrena　　　　aitortzera　　joan　zenean,　apaizak
Next-the　　　to confess-in order to　go　　did　　the priest
The next time　　(aitort-zera)

galdetu zion:
　ask　　to him-did

—Ia　　　zazpigarrenean...　　Ezer　ostu　al
So　　　　(the) seventh-on　　　Anything　stolen　(question)
　　the seventh (biblical) commandment

duzu?
do you

—Ez jauna. Naia bai, izan dut, ostekoa.
No　　sir　Want　yes　have　I　　after

—Berdin da, berdin da. Ostu　edo　osteko　nahia
Equal　is　equal　is　Stolen　or　to steal　desire
　　That's the same

izan, berdin-berdin da. Ia,　ia,　nolakoa izan zen
have　the same　　is　Well　well　what kind　have　did

nahi hori.
want　that

—Hara jauna, nagusiari arkumea eraman behar nion
To there / sir / to the boss / lamb / brought / have to / I did

eta, nireak txikitxoak zeuden eta, beste borda
and / mine / little ones / were / and / other / hut

batean handiagoak ikusi nituen eta, handixe osteko
in one / bigger / saw / I did / and / rather big / to steal

gogoa etorri zitzaidan. Langa-sareraino ekartzen
desire / came / came to me / overwhelmed / brought

nuen baino ezin atera, eta bertan utzi nuen.
i did / than / couldn't / take out / and / there / left / I did

—Gizona, gizona... Hori barkatzeko duro
Man / man / That / to forgive / duro (historical coin)

erdi-banako bi meza atera beharrean zera.
half-coin / two / mass / take out / instead of / that

—Duroa eman behar, beraz?
(A) duro / give / have to / so

—Jakina.
Of course

—Orain ematea berdin al da?
Now giving equal (question) is
Can I also give it now

—Ez da beharrezkoa. Hurrengo batean emango
Not is necessary Next in one will give
Next time

didazu.
you give me

—Gaur ematea nahiago nuke.
Today giving preferred (I) would

—Nahi duzuna...
Desire what you have
If you wish so...

Pernandok, apaizak barkamena eman zionean,
Pernando priests forgiveness give when he did

eskua luzatu eta emakumeen aitor-tokian
the hand extend and (in the) women's place of confession

dagoen saretik duroa eskaini zion.
just like that (in the) net (the) coin offer he-did

—Hortik ez, hortik ez —esan zion apaizak.
From there not from there not say to him-did priest

—Bai jauna bai, hemendik.
Yes   sir   yes   from there

—Hortik   ezin   hartu dut, gizona.
From there   impossible   take   I have   man
                  I can take it

—Ah!...   Niri   ere   horixe   bera   gertatu   zitzaidan
Ah   To me   also   that exactly   itself   happen   it did to me

arkumearekin.
with the lamb

GATZA OTE ZEN GERO?

GATZA OTE ZEN GERO?
Salt   Maybe   Did   Then

Behin batean, Gatzagatik gatza ekartzeko agindu
Once   in a   Saltworks   salt   to bring   order
Once upon a time

zioten Pernandori. Astoa aurrean hartuta, han
they did   to Pernando   Donkey   in front of   having taken   there

joan zen tipi tapa, tipi tapa, Gatzaga
go   he did   lightly   clip-clop   lightly   clip-clop   Gatzaga

aldera. Gatz-zaku handi bat jarri zion astoari
towards   Salt bag   big   one   put   him did   on the donkey

bizkar gainean, eta tipi tapa, tipi tapa,
(his) back   over   and   lightly   clip-clop   lightly   clip-clop

berriz etxe-aldera.
again   homeward

Bidean **hiru** **ibai** **igaro** **behar** **zituzten,** **eta** **ez**
On the way — three — rivers — to pass — have to — they did — and — not

dakigu **nola** **izan** **zen,** **baina** **lehendabizikoan** **sartu**
know — how — (past) — it did — but — for the first time — entered

zirenean, **astoa** **txirristatu** **eta** **erori** **zen.** **Bapo**
when they did — donkey — slipped — and — fall — he did — Very well

zegok **gure** **gatza!**
there is — our — salt
there went

Erdia **baino** **gehiago** **urtu** **zen,** **eta**
Half — than — more — dissolved — did — and

lehen **baino** **pisu** **gutxiago** **zeramala** **laster**
(the) first — than — weight — less — carrying — soon
less weight than first

antz **eman** **zion** **astoak.**
semblance — give — him did — donkey
noticed

Busti **detelako** **duk** **bada** **hori** **—zion astoak**
Get wet — because — you do — so — that — him did — donkey
So that happens when you get wet — figured the donkey

bere **kasa—** **busti** **detelako.** **Hori** **besterik** **ez**
its — on own — get wet — because — That — something else — not
on its own — because he got wet

ba	duk	berriz	ere	bustiko	diagu	bada..."	Eta
well	you do	again	also	wet	we have	so	And

bigarren	ibaian	zapla!	berriz	astoa	bera,	eta
the second	river	zap / right away	again	donkey	itself	and

hirugarrenean	berriz.	Hirugarrenetik	irten	zenean,
third time	again	From the third	come out	did

arin	eta	pozik	zihoan	gure	astotxoa.
quickly	and	happy content	he was going	our	little donkey

Arrano	astoa!	Nirekin	ibili	haiz	maltzurkeriak
Eagle / What the devil	donkey	With me	walk	you will	cunning

ikasi	dituk	hik	ere,	baina	oraindik	ez	haiz
learn	you will	you	also	but	still	not	you are

hire	nagusia	haina.	Bihar	emango	diat	nik
your	boss	so much / as much as your boss	Tomorrow	will give	it to you	I

hiri...
to you (emphasis)

Hurrengo	egunean,	tipi	tapa,	tipi	tapa,
Next	on the day	lightly	pitter-patter	lightly	pitter-patter

berriz Gatzagara. Hartu zuen Pernandok zaku handi
again   Saltville   Took   did   Pernando   sack   big

bat, esponjaz bete bete egin zuen, astoari
one   sponges   full (of)   full (of)   (emphasis)   it was   at the donkey

bizkar gainean jarri zion, eta... kaixo motel!
(his) back   over   put   to him did   and   hello   friend

—Gaur karga txikia diagu —zion astoak—.
Today   load   small   we have   to him did   donkey

Hala ere,   txikia baino txikiagoa
That way also   small than smaller
Even so   even smaller

hobe izango diagu.
better   have   we have
would be even better

Eta ibaira iristean, zapla! erori zen. Baina,
And   the river   upon arriving   splash!   fall   did   But

arranotan! oraingoan, karga gutxitu beharrean
hell!   this time   load   reduce   instead of
(exclamation)

gehiagotu egin zitzaion. Bigarren ibaian zakua
increased   (emphasis)   did to him   The second   river   sack

busti zuen berriz, eta gehiagotu oraindik.
get wet did again and increased still

Hirugarrenean, zakua busti zuen... eta indarrak
Thirdly sack get wet did and strength

behar ziren gero huraxe eramateko. Damutu
have to they did then that one to transport Regret

zitzaion horregatik: ez zuen harek gehiago
did to him for that reason not did that more

kargarik bustiko.
burden carry

Orduaz geroztik, gatza ondo lehor ekartzen zuen
Per hour since salt well dry brought did
Since then

bai Gatzagatik Pernandoren astoak. Busti, ez
yes for (the) Saltworks Pernando's donkey Get wet not

busti, zalantzan egoten zen batzuetan, baina...
get wet in doubt they are did sometimes but

gatza ote zen gero? esponjak ote ziren gero?
salt maybe he did then sponges maybe they did then

A ZER SARTUALDIA!...

A ZER SARTUALDIA!...
Ah What   Entry-Period
  A Small

Pernando neguan Adunara joaten omen zen
Pernando   in winter   to Aduna   to go   it is said   he did

bere ardiekin.
his   with sheep
with his sheep

Oso barruti on bat bai omen zegoen Adunan:
Very   area   nice one   yes   supposedly   there was   in Aduna
    It's a very nice area   indeed   there

itxia, ardiak errez zaintzekoa. Baina jabeak ez
closed   sheep   easy   to care for   But   the owner   not
closed off   easy to care for the sheep

omen zion Pernandori saldu nahi, eta, oi
supposedly   to him did   to Pernando   sell   want   and   oh
                            rent

den bezala, hilabeteko hainbestean eman ere ez:
is   like   one month   for as much   give   also   not

sartu-aldiko **honenbestean** **eman** **nahi** **omen**
entry-period for · as much as · give · want · it is said

zion.
to him did

Jabeak **hala** **nahi** **zuen** **ezkero,** **Pernandok**
The owner · that way · want · he did · since · Pernando
The owner wanted it that way

hartu dio, **bada,** **barruti hori** **sartu-aldi bakoitzean**
take · says · so · district · that · entry-time · each-on
accepts · · that area · · for each entry

hainbesteko bat **ordaintzekotan,** **eta**
such-amount · one · in payment · and
an amount

sartu ditu ardiak.
enter · has · sheep
he has his sheep enter

Sartu **bai,** **baina** **atera** **ez.** **Egunak** **igaro** **eta**
Entered · yes · but · take out · not · Days · spent · and

egunak **igaro** **eta** **ardiak** **ateratzen** **ez** **zituela**
days · spent · and · sheep · out · not · having them

ikusi **zuenean,** **nagusia** **joan** **zaio** **Pernandori** **oso**
see · when he did · (the) boss · went · is · to Pernando · very

haserre.
angry

—Gizona, ardi oiek ez al dituzu atera
Man sheep those not (question) you have take out

behar ala?
have to or

—Hori neronek ikusiko dut.
That myself will see have
I will have to see

—Zerorrek? Orduan barrutia zurea dela esan
What? Then district yours is-that say

liteke.
could be

—Nik ardiak atera artean bai behintzat.
I sheep take out between yes at least

Jabea sututa, joan da Tolosako lege-gizonarengana,
Owner quickly went is Tolosa from law-man to
to a lawyer from Tolosa

esan dio zer gertatzen zaion eta deitu diote,
say says what is happening to it-is made and called they say
tells him

Pernandori.
to Pernando

Lege-gizonak   galdetu zion:
Law-men(The) lawyers   asked   did

—Baina   barruti   hori   zenbat   hilabeterako,   edo
But   district   that   how many   for a month   or

zenbat   asterako   edo   zenbat   eguneroko   edo
how many   weeks   or   how many   for days   or

zenbat   ordurako   hartu   zenduan?
how many   by then   take   you were

—Ez   jauna,   ez...   Ez   dugu   ez   ordurik,   ez
No   sir   no   Not   is   not   (an) hour   not
            (lit. we have)

denbora   jakinik...   Sartualdiko   hainbestean   hartu
(in) time   specific   (The) entry period   meanwhile   take

nuen,   ardiak   sartu   nituen   eta   hantxe
(I) did   sheep   entered   (I) did   and   right there

dauzkat nahikoa jan   artean.
(I) have   enough   food   until
while there is food

Lege-gizonak **arrazoia** **eman** **zion.** **Barruti-jabea**
(The) lawyer   reason   give   did   (The) landlord

hortzak **estu** **estu** **eginda,** **etxera** **isil** **isilik** **joan**
teeth   tightly   tightly   done   home   silent   silently   went

zen. **Eta** **Pernandok** **bost** **egunean** **eta** **bost** **gauean**
did   And   Pernando   five   day on   and   five   night on
                    for five days   for five nights

han **eduki** **zituen** **ardiak;** **nahi** **haina** **janez.**
there   keep   did   the sheep   want   so much   food
         kept   they wanted

EMAZTEA HITZIK GABE

EMAZTEA HITZIK GABE
Wife   A Word   Without

Egun batean, ez zeukaten etxean arbasta bat ere,
Day   in a   not   they had   home in   roughing one also
On one day   in the home kindling

eta egur bila mendira joan zen.
and wood looking for Translating...   go   he did

Egurra mozten hasi besterik ez zuen egin eta
Wood   cutting   started else   not did (emphasis) and

gazte pila bat agertu zen, eta esan zioten:
young pile one appeared did and say   they did
a fresh

—Pernando: gaur dagoen egunarekin mendian
Pernando   today is-that   with today   in the mountain

lanean?
working
to work

—Zer egun da ba, gaur?
What day is well today

—Azkarateko pestak, gizona.
The from Azkarate festivals man

—Arraie-arraia, eta hala duk.
Hell and devil and that way you do

Eta zegoena zegoen tokian utzi eta Azkaratera
And was was place left and to Azkaratera

gazte haiekin joan zen.
young with those go he did

Etxean hartu beharrean baziren, ondo jaioak
Home take instead of they did well went out

zeuden.
were

Lau egunean ez zen etxeratu. Bosgarrenean etorri
Four on the day not did went home Fifth time come
For four days he didn't come home On the fifth

zen, eta emazte gajoa soroan lanean aurkitu zuen.
he did and wife poor field in at work find did
the poor wife at work in a field found

Alderatu zitzaion eta emaztea kopeta ilunarekin
Approach · did to her · and · wife · frowned · with darkness

isilik. Lehiatu zen emazteak zerbait esaten ote
silently · Give haste · he did · (to his) wife · something · saying · maybe

zion, baina alperrik, Emakume arren albotik ez
to him did · but · in vain · the Woman · despite · side · not

zuen hitz bat entzun.
did · word · one · heard

Orduan erretorearengana joan zen.
Then · to the rector / to the priest · go · he did

—Jauna —esan zion—. Etxean oker handiak
Sir · say · to him did · House in / At home · (a) problem · great

ditugu. Emaztea hitzik gabe daukat.
(we) have · Wife · not a word · without · (I) have

—Gizona, gizona...
Man · man

—Egin ditudan ahaleginak alperrik izan dira. Hitz
Made · I have · efforts · in vain · be / were · are · Word

bat   ezin   atera   zaio.
one   couldn't take out   is

—Emakumea, eta hitzik ez... ez zegok ondo.
The woman   and a word not   not there is   well
                                  that's not good

—Hala   esan liteke.
That way   say   could be
You can say that

—Goazen, goazen, zerbait   egin   beharko   dela
 Let's go   let's go   something (emphasis)   have to   is-that

 uste   dut.
thought   have

Joan ziren sorora,   eta emazteak   erretorea ikusi
Go   were   sister   and (his) wife   rector   see

 zuenean   hasi zen:
when she did   start   did
               she said

—Erretore jauna, berorri ere alderdi hauetatik?
 Rector   sir   to you   also   party   from these
 Priest   were you also part of this?

Eta Pernandok:
And   Pernando

—Orain etorri zaio hitza. Sendatu da.
Now   come   is   word   Healed   is

BAT EMAN, BESTEA HARTU

BAT EMAN, BESTEA HARTU
One Give The other Take

Gure zorioneko Pernando hau bazebilen behin
Our lucky Pernando this was walking once

beste askotan bezala, zer janik ez zuela.
other many times as what eaten anything not having

Halakoetan, jakina!, erretore jaunarengana joan
In such cases of course (the) rector the priest to the gentleman go

behar eskean.
have to asking

—Erretore jauna: anega bat harto emango balit
Rector Priest sir bread (fanega) one (of) corn will give if

"estimatuko" nioke ba...
appreciate I would well

—Anega bat arto?   Ez   zeukeat   nik   alperrentzat
Bread   one   corn   Not   have   I   for the fools
   A corn bread?

artorik.   Lan   egin   zak,   eta   hala   izango   duk
corn-any   Work   do   must   and   that way   have   you do

artoa.   Pernando   isil   isilik   etxeratu   zen.   Garizuma
bread   Pernando   silent   silently   went home   did   Lent

iritsi   zenean,   ordea,   erretoreari   "peatu"   behar
arrived   did   however   to the rector   confess   must

ziola,   eta   joan   zen   sakristiara   txartel   bila.
he said   and   go   he did   to the sacristy   (a) certificate   looking for
   (of faith)

—Ia   Pernando: zer   esan   nahi   du   Santuen
Well   Pernando   what   say   want   does   in Saints

komunioak?
communion

—Artorik   ematen   ez   duena   eramango   duala
Corn-any   giving   not   having   will carry   that
   Whoever does not give corn   will be taken by

infernuko   demonioak.
hell's   demons

—Utzi akiok bakean infernuko demonioari.
Leave those in peace hell's demons-to
Leave those hell demons in peace

Espiritu santua hartu behar duk laguntzat,
spirit holy took have to you do as help
You have to take the holy spirit as help

Espiritu santua; ez demonioa. Zer obra egin zikan
spirit holy not demon What work do with
the holy spirit did you do with

Espiritu santuak?
spirit holy
the holy spirit?

—Etxe bat Errenterian, jauna. ("Espiritu Santua"
House a in Errenteria sir Spirit Holy
A house

deitzen zioten etxe egile bat bizi zen orduan
called they did house builder one live he did time in
they called it a house builder lived at that time

Errenterian).
in Errenteria

—Bai eh? Joan adi bada Errenteriko Espiritu
Yes hey Go attentively so to Errenteria Spirit
Is that so?

santuarengana, eta eskatu hakiok txartela, nik
holy to and ask these certificates of faith I

behintzat ez diat emango eta.
at least   not I will will give then

Isildu zen berriz Pernando. Ez horregatik buru
Returned he did again   Pernando   Not for that reason head

makurturik gelditu.
bowed   stop

Bere baratzean bi kalabaza handi zituen erretore
His in the garden two pumpkins big he had priest

jaunak. Haiek baino handiagorik inguruetan ez
the gentleman Them than bigger any around not

zela eta, harro samar hitz egiten zuen, eta bai
was and proudly rather word doing did and yes
              talk about

ondo pozik erakutsi ere.
well happy show also

Joan zen Pernando erretore-etxera, eta neskameari
Go did Pernando   rectory and maid to
          the parish   (dative)

esan zion:
say he did

—Haizan, Mañaxi: erretore jaunak apustua egin din
In the air Manyaxi (the) priest sir bet do made
Hey

Eulizarreko Joxerekin, ia zeinek kalabaza
from Eulizarre with Joxerekin to see which pumpkin

handiagoa ekarri. Eta baratzean daukan handiena
bigger brings And in the garden has largest

emateko esan zidan.
to give say from me

—Hator baratzera, eta herorrek ebaki ezak
Come garden and roots cut (command)

handiena hara, pareta-kontrako huraxe duk.
largest to there wall-facing that one you do

Pernandok "rast!" ebaki, eta bizkarrean hartuta
Pernando rip cut and on the back having taken

eraman zuen.
carry he did

Erretore jauna etorri zenean:
(The) priest sir came did

—Eta zeinek irabazi du apustua erretore?
And which win has bet priest

Eulizarreneko Joxek ez zuen gauza handirik
From Eulizarrene Joseph not he did thing much any

ekarriko behintzat...
bring at least

—Baina zer esaten ari zera, Mañaxi?
But what saying -ing that Manyaxi

Mañaxik guztia esan zionean, erdi haserre,
Manyaxi everything say when she did half angry

erdi-parrez gelditu zen erretorea.
half-amused stop he did (the) priest

—Kalabaza zalea da horregatik Pernando alproja
Pumpkin fan of is for that reason Pernando lazy

hori. Txarteletan galanta eman diot bada baino
that Certificate of faith enormous give I say so than

berak handiagoa eraman dit...
he (the) bigger brought to me

OILASKO-HEZURRAK

OILASKO-HEZURRAK
Chicken-bones

Behin, etxeratu zenean, ez zegon ez surik eta
Once come home when he did not was not any fire and

ez bazkaririk. Nola, orduan, otordua egin? Ona
not any lunch How then meal make Good

Pernandok zer asmatu zuen.
Pernando what guess he did

Errektore-etxe aldera joan ziren emaztea, eta biak
Rector's house towards go he-did with the wife and both
The priest's house

lasterka bizian, emaztea aurretik eta senarra
running life-in wife in front and husband
lively

atzetik, emaztea garrasika begiak ateratzen
behind wife furiously the eyes coming out

balizkiote bezela, senarra deiadarka eta zigor
as if / like / husband / shouting / and / punishment

bat eskuetan duela emaztea elbarritzeko zorian.
one / in hands / having / wife / to cripple / about to
to beat

Errektoreak emaztearen garrasiak entzun
Rector / the wife's / screams / heard

dituenean atarira atera da, eta Pernando bere
when he hears / hall / got out / is / and / Pernando / his

zigorrarekin ez egiteko bat egiteko antzean
punishment / not / to do / one / to do / pretending

ikusten duenean bien artean sartzen da oihu
see / when he does / both / between / entering / is / cry

eginez:
doing

—Geldirik! Gizona zer da zatarkeri hau?
Quiet / Man / what / is / nonsense / this

—Zer den? Hanelako emakumea, txiki-txiki eginda
What / is / such / the woman / little-little / done
very little

ere, ez da behar bezala ordaintzen.
also not is have to like paying

—Zer izan dezute bada?
What be have so

—Ezer ez.
Anything not

—Ta ezer ezengatik horrela jarri?
Why anything for that like that put

—Bai jauna: ezer ez, ez surik, ez bazkaririk.
Yes sir anything not not any fire not any lunch

—Begira, begira; gaurko behintzat zuentzako
Looking looking today's at least for you
I see I see

bazkaria nire etxean badago eta utzi zaiozute
lunch my home there is and leave you have to

haserreari.
(your) anger

Pernandok ez zuen besterik nahi, eta pozik
Pernando not did otherwise want and happy

haserre-itxura utzi zuan.
angry-looking   left   to him-did
stopped being angry

Emaztea sukaldera eraman zuten, eta Pernando
Wife   kitchen   brought   they did   and   Pernando

Erretore jaunarekin jan-gelara bildu zen.
Rector   sir   dining room   gathered   did
priest

Errektoreak txuliatzeko gogo handia zeukan egun
Rector   to polish   desire   great   he had   day
The priest

hartan, eta bazkaritan oilaskoa ekarri zutenean,
in that   and   for lunch   chicken   bring   when they did

hezurrak Pernandoren aldera jarri zituen eta
bones   Pernando's   towards   put   did   and

mamiak berera.
crumbs   the same

Errektorea parrez gur-gur zegoen Pernandok
Rector   by the way   laughing   was   Pernando
The priest

jartzen zuen aurpegi iluna ikusirik, eta, zerbait
putting   did   face   dark   having seen   and   something

esan behar bada, eta esan zion:
say have to so and say him did

—Aztian emaztea harrapatu izan bazenu, zer
Had wife caught (past) if what

egingo zenion?
will do to her-would

—Jauna: orain plater honekin egiten dudan bezala
Sir now dish with this doing do as

lepoa bihurrituko nion.
neck twist I did

Eta platerari buelta emanaz, mamiak bere aldera
And platter round by turning (the) scraps his towards

ekarri eta hezurrak errektoreari utzi zizkion.
bring and bones rector left he did

ELKAR EZIN IKUSI!

ELKAR   EZIN   IKUSI!
Each other Impossible   To See
They couldn't stand each other!

Asto   itdu bat zeukan Pernandok ikuiluan.
Donkey   had   one   he had   Pernando   in the stable
          Pernando had a donkey in the stable

Asto   hura inork erosiko ez   ziola,   amezketar
Donkey that nobody   buy   not he said   from Amezketa
         Nobody would buy that donkey

guztiek   bazekiten.
everyone   knew

Zertarako erosiko zion, bada, inork asto   itsua?
What for   buy   did   so   nobody donkey blind
Why would anyone buy a blind donkey?

Halako batean, Pernandok berak erosi zuen   beste
Such   in a   Pernando   he   buy   he did (an) other
        Once

asto   bat, eta... itsua   ura   ere!
donkey one   and   blind   that one also
                            (hura)

Pernando gizajoa txoratuko zela   uste izan   zuten
Pernando   poor   crazy   would   think (past) they did
Pernando would have gone completely crazy

amezketarrak.   Baina... bai zera txoratu!
by those of Amezketa   But   yes that   go crazy
As if he went crazy! He didn't...

Hurrengo peri eguna etorri zenean, hartu   zituen
Next   fair   day   came   did   took   (he) did
(plural object)

bi   asto   itsuak eta han joan zen Tolosara.
two donkey(s) blind and there go   did Tolosa to

Gerturatu zen bat.
Get close   did   one
Someone approached him

—Asto horiek saltzeko   al   dauzkazu, Pernando?
Donkey those for sale (question)   have   Pernando

—Halaxe   dauzkat   bada.
Like that   (I) have (them)   so
(plural object)

—Ez daukate itxura txarra... Ez   al   dute
Not have-not   looks   bad   Not (question) they do
they have

akatsik?
mistake any
any defect

—Ez, ez... Denbora askotxoan elkarrekin ikuilu
No   No   (in) time   quite a while   together   together

batean egon direla eta... elkar ezin-ikusia,
in a   stay   are-that   and   each other   impossible-to see
  stable   they can't stand

besterik ez.
else   not
otherwise

—Hori besterik ez baldin bada...
That   else   not   if   so

—Besterik ez. Ezin elkar ikusi...
Else   not   Couldn't   each other   saw

Beste gizajoak erosi zituen bi asto horiek, dirua
Other   people   bought   did   two   donkey   those   money

eman zion Pernandori, eta amezketarra han joan
give   did   to Pernando   and   from Amezketa   there   go

zen pozik diruari txin txin eraginez.
he did   happy   money   jingling   clink   by influence
    content   because of

Eroslea ere alai zegoen, astoak merke xamar
(The) buyer   also   happy   was   donkey   cheap   quite

erosi zituela eta. Baso-erdi bat jesus batean
bought having them and Half-forest one beginning one in

ziplatu eta gero, hasi zen etxe-alderako
drink and then started did homeward

asmotan. Astoei soka kendu zieten, eta
with the intention Donkeys from shoes remove did and

arre esanaz, hasi zen txistu jotzen.
go saying started did whistle playing

Astoak geldi ordea. Makilaz jota ibiltzen
Donkey still however Wanderers walking walking
not moving

asten baziren, beti bazterretara eta behar ez zen
used to they did always margins and have to not did

tokietara zihoazen. Zer asto arrano ziren
places went What donkey eagle did
what the devil

haiek!
they

Begira eta begira, itsuak zirela antz eman
Looking and looking blind they were semblance give

153

zion azkenerako erosleak. Eta eginahaletan han
did · eventually · to the buyers · And · everywhere in · there

joan zen Pernandoren bila.
go · did · Pernando's · looking for

—Baina gizona —esan zion aurkitu zuenean— zer
But · man · say · he did · find · when he did · what

asto eman dizkidazu? zertarako ditut nik asto
donkey · give · you-to me · what for · have · I · donkey

horiek, elkar ere ezin ikusi dutela?
those · each other · also · impossible couldn't · see · that they have

Ekarriazu niri berriz dirua eta hartu itzazu zure
Bring · to me · again · money · and · take · leave them · your

asto zahar horiek!...
donkey · old · those

—Ez "konpañero" ez. Astoak erosi baino lehen, nik
No · companion · no · Donkeys · buy · than · (the) first · I

argi asko esan nizun elkar ezin ikusi
clear · many · say · I had you · each other · impossible couldn't · see

zutela.   Hala   ere   erosi   egin   zizkidazun.
them having   That way   also   bought   (emphasis)   to me-did

Orain...   hor   konpon!   Ibiltzeko   gauza   ez   badira,
Now   there   fix   To walk   thing   not   there are

lukainkak   egiteko   saldu   itzazu.
sausages   to do   sell   leave them

ERRETOREAREN TXERRIA

ERRETOREAREN TXERRIA
The Priest's   Pig

Orduan   ere,   urtero   bezala,   Amezketako   erretore
Then   also   annually   as   (the) Amezketa of   priest
In that time

jaunak   txerria   hil   zuan.   Txikia   zen   ordea,   eta
sir   pig   killed   to him-did   Small   did   however   and
                                 It was small

ohiturari   jarraituaz,   etxerik   etxe   odolki
custom   following   house any   house   blood sausage
    according to custom   house by house

zabaltzen   hasi   balitz,   beretzat
extending   start   if he were   for himself
  giving out   if he would start

batere   gabe   geldituko   zen.   Ez   banatzea,   berriz,
any   without   get   he did   Not   distributed   again
    he wouldn't get any   To not share   however

txartzat   hartuko   zuten   herrian.   Zer   egingo   eta
as bad   take   they did   in the village   What   will do   and
  people would see as bad

zer ez egingo, Pernandori deitu zion eta
what not will do To Pernando call him did and

gertatzen zitzaiona esan zion.
happening what was tell him did

—Horrek erremedio erreza dauka, erretore jauna.
That remedy simple have rector sir
priest

—Ia bada, ia...
Indeed so indeed

—Hil duan txerri txiki hori jarri beza baratza
Killed will pig small that put let gate

aldeko ate-ondoan guztiek ikusi dezaten.
in favor of gate-side in everyone see that they

—Bai...
Yes

—Eta bihar esan beza, ostu egin
And tomorrow say let stolen (emphasis)

diotela.
to me-have done

157

—Arrano arranoa... Ez zegok gaizki... Apaiz batek
Eagle   eagle in   Not there is   wrong   Priest   one
    What the devil

gezurra esatea ez duk egoki, baina... gauza
lying   telling   not you do appropriate but   thing

gutxi duk, eta horixe egingo diat...
few   you do and exactly! will do   I will

Esan bezala, jarri zuen txerria baratza aldeko ate
Say   as   put   he did   pig   garden   for   door

ondoan. Eta gauean, Pernandok berak ostu zion.
side in   And   at night   Pernando   he   steal him did

Hurrengo   goizean,   txerria han ez zegoela
Next   in the morning   pig   there not   was

erretoreak ikusi zuenean, estututa deitu zion
the priest   see   when he did   worried   call   him did

Pernandori, eta esan zion:
to Pernando   and   say   him did

—Pernando ez dakizu zer gertatu zaidan! Gaur
Pernando   not   know   what happen   it is to me Today

gauean txerria eraman ez didate bada?...
at night pig brought not they have so

—Hori, hori. Horixe esan behar du: harrapatu
That that Exactly! say have to does caught

egin diotela.
do they say
(emphasis)

—Ez dela gezurra, Pernando. Benetan harrapatu
Not is-that lying Pernando Really caught

didate.
they have

—Hori, hori. Eutsi hitz horri. Horrela esan ezkero,
That that Hold on word that Like that say since

guztiek sinestuko diote.
everyone believe they say

Esan eta esan, Pernandok ere sinestu zion
Say and say Pernando also believe him did

azkenik.
finally

—Hori hala bada, erretore jauna, nire etxean
That thus so priest sir my home

begiratu dezatela lehendabizi.
look let them look first

—Ez gizona. Zure errezelorik ez daukat nik.
No man Your complaints not have I

—Ez dio ardura. Nere etxeko baztar guztiak ikusi
Not says care My house's corners all see

ditzatela.
let them

Eta ikusi behar izan zituzten. Jo gora eta jo
And see have to (past) they did Hit up and hit

behera han ibili ziren, baina ez zen txerririk
down there walk they did but not did pigs

agertu.
appeared

Ez zen erreza, ondo ezkutatuta zegoen eta.
Not did simple well hiding was and

Haurraren sehaskan, lastairan sartuta zeukaten;
The child's / cradle / in the blanket / inserted / they had

haurra berriz, negarrez sehaskan eta Pernandoren
child / again / crying / cradle / and / Pernando's

emaztea kantari, sehaskari eragiten. Zeni
wife / singing / cradle / create / Would

bururatuko zitzaion sehaska arren barruan, haur
occur to / did to him / cradle / despite / inside / child

azpian begiratzea?
under / watching

Garizuma etorri zen, ordea, eta aitortzerakoan
Lent / came / did / however / and / confessing

erretoreari guztia esan behar. Esan zion, eta
to the priest / everything / say / have to / Tell / him did / and

erretoreak, egia jakiteak ematen zion
the priest / truth / knowing / give / him did

pozaren pozez, guztia barkatu zion Pernando
(with) happy's / happy / everything / forgive / him did / Pernando
with happiness

azkarrari.
clever

BI ASTO

BI   ASTO
Two   Donkey(s)

Pernandoren burua nola ote   zebilen egun hartan!
Pernando's   head   how   maybe   he was   day   in that
How was Pernando's head that day?

Astoa aurrean   hartuta
Donkey in front of having taken
With the donkey in front

joan zen   goizean   feriara,   eta
go   did in the morning to the fair   and
he went to the fair in the morning

astoa   non   zuen ez   zekiela
the donkey where he was not knew-that
without knowing where the donkey was

zetorren gauean etxera.
was coming at night home
he came back home at night

Asto   gabe   zetorrela   ikustean emazteak zer
Donkey without (he) was coming upon seeing (his) wife what

esango ote zion, beldur zen. Geldi-geldi,
will tell maybe her did fear he did Still-still
Completely still

bere kasa itz eginez, burua alde batera eta
his on own word making head side together and
thinking of what to say

bestera erabiliaz zihoan etxe-aldera.
to another using he was going homeward

Ostatu-aurrera hala iristen ikusi zuenean,
The inn-in front thus reached see he did-in

ostalariak esan zion:
(the) innkeepers say him did

—Zer duzu, Pernando, horrela etortzeko? zerbait
What do you Pernando like that to come something

gertatu al zaizu?
happened (question) to you-has

—Bai gizona. Astoa feriara eraman dut, eta ferian
Yes man Donkey to the fair brought have and market

ahaztuta ez nator bada? Oraindik horrelakorik...
forgotten not come so Still something like that

Tokitan dago, hura orain arren bila joateko.
Very far / is / that / now / despite / looking for / to go

Zorioneko astotzar hori... emango nioke!...
Lucky / lucky / that / will give / I would

—Utzi ezazu bihar arte, gizona. Bihar
Leave / do it(command) / tomorrow / until / man / Tomorrow

ere han egongo da bai.
also / there / will be / is / yes

—Bai, hori bai, ondo lotuta utzi dut eta. Baina nire
Yes / that / yes / well / tied / left / have / and / But / my

emazteari zer esango diot? Egia esaten badiot...
wife / what / will tell / will give / True / saying / if I tell

—Gezurra esan. Esaiozu... esate baterako... Hara.
(A) lie / say / Try / to say / for a time / To there
say for example

Zure lagun batek txahal txikidun behi bat erosi
Your / help / a / calf / small / cow / one / bought

duela: txahal txiki hori ezin eramanik aurkitu
having / calf / small / that / couldn't / carry / find

duzula bidean, eta txahala gainean hobeto eraman
you have / on the way / and / calf / over / better / brought

dezan, astoa eskatu dizula eta bihar berriz
so he can / donkey / ask / you say / and / tomorrow / again

ekartzekotan eman egin diozula.
to bring back / give / do(emphasis) / you say

—Ez zera makala, adiskide! Buru iaioa daukazu
Not / that / joke / friend / Head / teacher / have

gero gauzak asmatzeko! Nere Mari-Joxepari egia
then / things / invent / My / Mary-Joseph / truth

esan behar izan banio, istiluak izango ziren gure
say / must / be(past) / I am / troubles / have / did / our

etxean... Horrela, ordea... bapo zegok!
home / Like that / however / very well / there is

Uste bezala gerta. Sartu zen Pernando etxera,
Think / how / (it) happens / Entered / did / Pernando / home

astoa non zuen galdetu zion Mari-Joxepak,
donkey / where / he was / asked / him did / Mary-Joseph

lagunari   nola   eman   zion   erantzun   zion
to his friend   how   give   him did   answer   her did

Pernandok,   Mari-Joxepak   sinestu   zion...   itxuraz
Pernando   Mary-Joseph   believe   him did   apparently

behintzat,   eta   bake   santuan   oheratu   ziren.
at least   and   peace   holy-in   go to bed   they did

Hurrengo   goizean   joan   zen   gure   gizona   feria
Next   morning-in   go   did   our   man   market

tokira   asto   bila...   eta   han   astorik   ez.
to the place   donkey   looking for   and   there   donkey-any   not

Hara   bigarren   istilua,   eta   bigarren   gezurra   asmatu
There,   (a) second   incident   and   (a) second   lie   invent

beharra!
the need

Etxeratu   zenean
Come home   when he did

—Astoa   ez   al   dakarrek,   Pernando?
Donkey   not   (question)   bring   Pernando

—Hara, ez bada. Atzo, txahala gainean zuela
Then see / not / so / Yesterday / cart / over / having

bidean zihoala, behiak bultzada bat egin
on the way / as he went / cows / push / a / (emphasis)

omen zion eta elbarrituta dago. Ni ikusi
it is said / did / and / distressed / is / Me / saw

nauenean etorri nahi izan du gaixoak, baina
when saw me / came / want / (past) / does / sick people / but

gaizkiagotu ez dadin nire adiskidearen ukuiluan
worsen / not / may / my / friend's / in the barn

bertan utzi dut egun batzuetarako. San
there / left / have / day / in some / St

Bartolometarako hemen izango dugu.
for Saint Bartholom / here / have / is
(lit. we have)

Pernando hizketan ari zela, bere astoa ukuiluan
Pernando / talking / -ing / was / his / donkey / in the barn

arrantzaka hasi zen.
braying / started / did

—Ah kirtena!... —esan zion Mari-Joxepak
Ah   the handle   say   him did   Mary-Joseph

senarrari—. Aditzen al duk ori? Gezurrak
to the husband   Understand   (question)   you do   that   Lies

asmatzeko ere burua behar dik, burua; ez hik
to invent   also   head   have to   to you   head   not   you

hor lepo-gainean daukaken lapiko zahar hori. Bi
there   on the hill   has   pot   old   that   Two

asto zeuzkeagu guk etxean, bi asto.
donkey   stay   we   home   two   donkey

—Bi?
Two

—Bi, bai, bi: atzo ezkeroztik ukuiluan dagoen
Two   yes   two   yesterday   since   in the barn   is-that

hori eta hi.
that   and   you

Aurreko egunean Pernando bera baino
(In the) previous   on the day   Pernando   himself   than

lehenago	ez	zen	bada	astoa	etxera	etorri!	Bai
earlier	not	did	so	donkey	home	came	Yes

Mari-Joxepak	ukuiluan	isil	asko	sartu	ere.	Toki
Mary-Joseph	in the barn	silent	many	entered	also	Place

onean	zeuden	Pernando	gizajoaren	ziriak!
good-in	were	Pernando	poor man's	shouts

TXALBURUDUN ARDOA

TXALBURUDUN ARDOA
Tadpole-with   Wine

Bera   **bezalako**   **erreminta jenero batekin,**
Himself   like   (a) tool   sort of   with one
                 engaging himself like a tool

ari eta ari zen Pernando ardotegi-zulo batean,
work and work did   Pernando   wine cellar   in one
    working

zurrut eta zurrut. Makina bat baso erdi zor zituen
drink   and   drink   Machine   one   glass   half   debt   he had
   constantly drinking   A lot of half glasses of

etxe hartan,   **eta**   **hala**   **ere,**
house   in that   and   that way   also
   in that house

zorrak ordaindu beharrean,   **edan eta edan,**
debts   pay   instead of   drink   and   drink
   instead of paying his debts   drinking all the time

gehiagotu egiten zituen zor horiek.
increased   doing   he had   debt   those
he increased his debt

Estutasun hartatik nola aterako eta nola aterako,
Distress from that how come out and how come out
as he came out

hara zer gogoratu zitzaion.
to there what remember did to him
then somethinghe thought of

Irten zen ardotegitik, joan zen inguruetako
Come out did winery from went did nearby

putzu-zulo batera, eta zortzi hamarren bat txalburu
waterhole together and eight tenths a tadpoles
eighty

harrapatuta, atzera sartu zen. Ezkutuan, sartu
caught back enter did Secretly enter

zituen bi txalburu basoan, eta gainerakoak
did two tadpoles in the glass and the rest

botilan. Handik pixka batera...
in the bottle From then on (a) little together
After a little while

—Zer zikinkeri arrano da hau?
What dirty eagle is this
mess

—Zer da, zer da?...
What is what is

—Horrelakorik ez zaio gizonari egiten.　　　Ardoa
Something like that　not　is　to the man　doing　　　Wine
　　　Don't do something like that to a man

eskatu eta zikinkeri hau ekarri.
asked　and　filth　this　bring

Tabernaria gerturatu zen.
Tavern host　get close　did
　　　approached

—Haizu, Pernando, nik ez dut zikinkeriarik ematen,
Hey　Pernando　I　not have　filthiness　give(n)

eh, eta kontu zer esaten duzun. Hobe zenuke zor
hey　and　care　what　saying　you have　Better　enough　debt

duzun ardoa ordaindu.
you have　wine　pay

—Ardoa, ardoa　al　da bada hau?
Wine　wine　(question)　is　so　this

—Zer ote da bada?
What　maybe　is　so

—Ur　zikina　besterik　ez;
Water　dirt　else　not

putzu zikinetik ekarritako ura.
puddle   dirty   brought   water
you brought water from a dirty puddle

—Kontuz gero, zer esaten duzun...
Careful   then   what   saying   you have
with what you are saying

—Kontuz? Txalburu bat irentsita gero kontu?
Careful   Tadpole   one   swallowed   then   care
I should be careful

—Zer txalburu eta txalburu-ondo gero! Txoratu
What   tadpole   and   tadpole-good   then   Crazy

egin zera, gizona...
(emphasis)   that   man

—Txoratu eh? Eta hau, zer da hau?
Crazy   hey   And   this   what   is   this

Ontzian zeuzkan bi txalburuak
In the pitcher   he had-that   two   tadpoles
The two tadpoles he had in the pitcher,

erakutsi zizkionean, harrituta gelditu zen
show   when he was them   surprised   stop   did
when he showed them,

ardo saltzailea.
(the) wine   seller

—Jakina! —zion Pernandok panparroi— putzuko
Of course / did / Pernando / showy / from the puddle

ur zikina, bota diozu eta, txalburuak etorri...
water / dirty / throw / you say / and / tadpoles / come

Botilan ere izango dira gehiago onenean...
Will be / also / have / are / more / at best

Bai, baziren. Botilako ardoa itzultzean, han irten
Yes / they did / Bottle / wine / returning turning over / there / come out

zen beste txalburu-mordoxka bat.
did / other / tadpole(s)-group / one

Eta Pernandok:
And / Pernando

—Hau ezin isilik eraman liteke. Ardoari ur
This / couldn't / silently / brought / could be / To the wine / water
This can't be kept quiet

zikina botatzea...
dirty / to throw

—Hara bada, Pernando, sekulan ez diot bada
There / then / Pernando / never / not / I have / so

175

botatzen. Gaur... bai... pixka-pixka bat. Baina ur
throw(n)   Today   yes   little little   a   But   water
just a little bit

garbi, ederra zelakoan...
clear   beautiful   I thought

—Niri ez didazu bada berriz horrelakorik
To me   not   you give me   then   again   something like that

egingo.   Nik parte emango dut,   eta
will do   I   part   will give   have   and
I will take my part

ikusiko dugu zer gertatzen den.
see   is   what   happening   is
we will see what happens

—Ez Pernando, ez. Zaude isilik.
No   Pernando   no   You are   silent
You will be

Hor gordeta daukadan   ardo zahar bikain
There   stored   have   wine   old   magnificent
I have stored   magnificent old wine

horretatik emango dizut gaurtik aurrera. Eta
from that   will give   (I) will to you   from today   forward   And

zor guztiak barkatuko dizkizut.
debt   all   forgive   to you-will forgive

Ondo isildu zen bai, Pernando.

Well   silent   did   yes   Pernando

And yes, Pernando was quiet

HIL, BARKATU, ETA PIZTU

HIL, BARKATU, ETA PIZTU
Die   Forgive   And   Revive

Nola edo hala   **artalde baten jabe izateko**
How or that way   flock   a   owner   to be
One way or another   to be the owner of a flock

gogoa sartu zitzaion Pernandori. Ardiak izan nahi,
desire entered did to him To pernando Sheep (past) want
was what Pernando started to desire   wanted

eta ardiak erosteko dirurik ez. Besteren bat
and sheep to buy any money not Someone else a

estutuko zen noski, baina ez gure Pernando.
tighten did of course but not our Pernando
would worry

Dirurik ez zuela? Geroago ordaintzekotan
Any money not having Later with intention of paying
On credit

erosi.
bought

Hala   erosi   zuen Pernandok bere artalde hori.
That way bought did   Pernando   his   flock   that

Egunak etorri eta egunak joan, ordaintzeko ordua
Days   come   and days   go   to pay   time

ere   etorri zen.
also come   did

Ez   zen estutu. Bi   adiskideren   bila   joan zen,
Not did worry   Two friends   looking for went did

eta:
and

—Eup!...
Hey!

—Zer   dugu,   Pernando?
What   we have Pernando
       is it

—Zera! Ardiak ordaintzeko eguna   etorri zaidala
So   Sheep   to pay   the day come   to me that it has
                                               has come to me

eta, nik dirurik   ez   dudala   eta, zuek
and   I   any money   not I have   and   you all

lagundu beharko didazuela...
  help   must   you will to me
must help me

—Guk? Gure diruak errez eramango dituzu.
  We   Our   moneys easily will carry you will (them)
          You would easily take our money

—Ez dut zuen diru beharrik.   Hitzezko
Not have did money need   Word-related
   I don't need money   Verbal

laguntasuna eskatzen dizuet, ez diruzkoa.
 friendship   asking for I (to) you all not monetary
  support   I'm asking you for

—Hori emango dizugu, bada, gizona.
 That   will give we will (to) you then   man

—Tira bada; goazen. Nere hartzekoduna
Alright   then   let's go   My the one to whom I owe
       (1st pers. plural imp.) (Nire)   creditor

 zain   dago onez gero, eta goazen.
on watch is   well after and let's go
 waiting   at this point

Han   zihoazen hirurak hartzekodunaren   bila.
There   went   all three the one to whom I owe looking for
             the creditor

Iturritxo baten ondotik igarotzerakoan, esan
Little spring one of beside from while passing by say

zien   Pernandok bere bi lagunei:
did to them   Pernando   his   two   friends

—Geldi bertan. Ni   hementxe   geldituko naiz. Zuek
Stop   there   Me   here-(emphasis)   stay-will   I am   You all
                  right here

   biok   zoazte,   eta   nire   diruaren
two-(emphasis)   go   and   my   money of
              (2nd pers. plural imp.)

zain   dagonarengana   iristen zaretenean, esan
on watch   is-of the one who-towards   arriving   you are-when   say
    to the one who is waiting   when you arrive

iezaiozue: "Pernando gizarajoa! Gurekin zetorren
you tell him/her   Pernando   poor guy!   With us   was coming

zuri   zorra   ordaintzera.   Izerdi-patsetan,   korrika
to you   debt   payment-to do-to   Sweat-covered in   running
          (-tzea verbal noun)

zetorren,   eta   iturrian   ur   hotza   edanda,
was coming   and   fountain-at   water   cold   having drunk

gaitzen batek   hartu   eta zerraldo gelditu da".
  illness   one   took   and motionless   stop   is
   some illness   got a hold of him   remained

—Baina gizona...
  But   man

—Zuek hori esan zazue,   eta
You all   that   say   (imperative)   and
    You (all) should say that!

gero-gerokoak.
  later-is for later
What comes after, comes after

Esan   eta   egin.   Hartzekoduna   han   zegoen
Say   and   done   The creditor   there   was

Pernandoren zain.
  Pernando for   waiting

—Hara   bada   —esan   zioten   Pernandoren   bi
Well   then   say   they did   Pernando's   two

adiskideak—.   Egin   ahala   guztian
  friends   Do   as much as   everything in
    He was doing his best

honeraxe   zetorren
here-exactly   he was coming
   coming right here

zor   dizun   dirua ekartzera.   Baina
(the) debt   you he owes   money   to bring   But
    to bring you the money he owes

iturritik   igarotzean,   izerditan zegoela
fountain-from   passing-when   sweat-in   that he was
   when passing a fountain   being all sweaty

ura edan du, eta plast!... luze-luze erosi da.
water drank has and splat long-long fall is
he drank water Fell stretched out

Azkenekotan dago noski.
Last-state being in is of course
He is in his last moments

—Gizarajoa!... Ia, ia, goazen, goazen agudo,
Poor guy! Come on come on let's go let's go quickly

ia zer-edo-zer egin dezakegun.
let's see what-or-what (emphasis) that we can
something or other (1st pers plural of ahal izan)

Pernando han zegoen iturri-ondoan bapo eserita,
Pernando there was by the spring very well sitting

baina bere hartzekoduna zetorrela ikusi
but his creditor (he) was coming saw

zuenean, lurrean luze-luze etzan zen, begiak
when he did earth-on stretched out lay down did the eyes
(his eyes)

itxi zituan, eta ahoa okertu ere bai... Hila zegoela
close was and mouth twist also yes Dead was

zirudien.
it seemed

Ardiak saldu zizkionak hala ikusi zuenean,
Sheep sell those to him gave that way saw when he did

kupituta, esan zuan:
astonished say to him-did

—Makina bat bar eragindako Pernando gizarajoa!...
Machine a wave caused by Pernando damn!

Hi ere hil behar hitzan eta hil haiz...
Hey! also killed have to in words and killed you will

Jaungoikoak barkatuko al dizkik zorrak, nik
(the) lord forgive (question) has debts I

barkatu diaten bezala...
forgive they say as

—Barkatzen al diozu zor zizuna?
Forgiving (question) you say debt you were

—Bai bada, gizarajoari.
Yes so to the poor man

Orduan, bat-batean altxa zen Pernando. Eta
Then suddenly stood up did Pernando And

hala   zion:
that way   did

—Zuek   testigu   eh?   Zorra   barkatzen   didala   esan
You   witnesses   hey   Debt to   forgiving   that   say

du.   Gero ukatzen badu, zuek testigu.
does   Then   denying   if   you   witness

185

ZAKURRAREN MUTURRA

ZAKURRAREN MUTURRA
Dog's   Muzzle

Behin batean, Pernando Amezketarra bazihoan ba
Once   in a   Pernando   from Amezketa   was going   well
Once upon a time   -

bide batean   barrena,   eta   gizon ondo jantzi bat,
road   on one   along   and   man   well   dress   a
   on a road   a well dressed man

orain euskeraz Kaballero deitzen den   oietako bat,
now   in Basque   gentleman   called   is   of those   one
                              is called   one of those

bere zakurrarekin aurkitu zuen.
his   dog-with   find   he did
    with his dog   encountered

Alderatu   zenean,   gizonak   ez   zion   zaunkarik
Moved aside   when he did   the man   not   did   bark-any

egin;   zakurrak ere   ezer   esan ez. Hau da, ez
(emphasis)   the dog   also anything   say not This is   not
                                        did not say That is to say

batak eta ez besteak ez zioten egun onik eman.
one and not the other not they did day good any give
give any greeting

Baina zakurra alderatu zitzaion, praka zarrak
But dog approach did to him trousers torn

usaindu zituen eta atzeko hanka altxatzen hasi zen.
smelled did and behind leg lifting start did

Orduan, Pernandok, zakurra uxatu zuen esanaz:
Then Pernando dog shoo away did say-while
drove away while saying

Oha hemendik, nagusiaren mutur horrekin.
Shoo from here the owner's snout with that
with that master's snout

Ordu-arte isilik egon bazan, jaun arrek
Time-until silently stay he had been man males
Until then not saying anything he remained the gentleman

bazuen orduantxe zer esana.
he had just then something sayable
to say

Arren albotik Pilatosen albotik baino
Of that one from the side (Pontius) Pilate's side than
From his side more than Pontius Pilate (said it)

zitalkeri zorrotz, min, latzagoak atera ziren.
insults sharp painful harsher take out did
a sharper, harsher more painful insults came out

Ez hori bakarrik; **handik egun gutxira, epaikari**
Not that alone   from there day soon (a) judge
And not just that happened   soon after that

aurrera deitu zuen Pernando.
forward call did Pernando
called up

Baso-erdi bat edateko garaia izango zen aldera
Glass-half one to drink time have did approximately
Half a glass

epaikariaren aurrean **bildu zirenean,**
judge in front of   gathered when they did
in front of the judge   when they gathered

Kaballero izeneko hura bere zakurrarekin, eta
(the) gentleman called that his dog-with and
the one called Kaballero   with his dog

Pernando txakur txiki bat ere gabe.
Pernando sip small one also without
not even

Berehala beren auziari eraso zioten.
Immediately their case-to attack they did
address directly

Jaunak:
(The) gentleman (said)

—Gizon honek, **orain egun gutxi**
Man this   now day few
This man   a few days ago

iseka   egin   zidan.
mocked (emphasis) to me he did
he mocked me

Pernandok:
Pernando

—Ez da egia.
Not   is   true

Epaikariak:
(The) Judge
(modern: Epaile)

—Tilin! Tilin! Tilin!
Ding!   Ding!   Ding!
(Judge calling for order)

Jaunak,   berriro:
Gentleman   again

—Gizon honek iraindu   egin   ninduen.
Man   this   insulted (emphasis) he did to me

Pernandok:
Pernando

—Ez da egia.
Not   is   true

Epaikariak:
(The) Judge
(modern: Epaile)

—Tilin! Tilin! Tilin!
Ding!   Ding!   Ding!

Azkenik, jaunak:
Finally   gentlemen

—Gizon   honek   esan   zidan,   zakurrak   nire
Man   this   say   to me he did   (that) the dog   my

muturra zuela.
snout   that it had

Pernandok:
Pernando

—Hori bai dela egia.
That   yes   is-that   true

Epaikariak:
(The) Judge
(modern: Epaile)

—Eta iraindu ez zenuela diozu?
And   insulted   not   insulted-not   you say

—Ez noski.
Not of course

—Nola ordea?
How however

—Hara epaikari jauna: Zakur hau, norena da?
To there young sir Dog this whose is

—Nagusiarena.
(The) master-belonging to
The owner's

—Eta zakur honen muturra?
And dog this snout
      this dog's

—Nagusiarena.
(The) master-belonging to
The owner's

—Hori da ba nik esan nuena. Zakurrak nagusiaren
That is well I say meant (The) dog owner's

muturra zuela.
snout that it had

Guztiak mututu ziran, ori entzun zutenean; eta,
All get silent they did that heard when they did and

horra, nola Pernando Amezketarrak   auzia   irabazi
there   how   Pernando   from Amezketa   the dispute   win

zuen.
did

ERREKTORAREN AMUARRAINAK

ERREKTORAREN AMUARRAINAK
(The) Rector's   Trout
The Priest's

Herriko   **Errektoreak**   **askotan**   **eramaten**   **zuen**
(The) town-of   Rector   often   took   he did
                   priest

Pernando   **berekin**   **bazkaltzera,**   **horrela**   **barre**
Pernando   with him   to lunch   in this way   laughter

nahikoa egitearren.
enough   in order to do
           to have

Behin   **batean**   **joan** **zan**   **bazkaltzera,**   **eta**   **entzun**
Once   in a   go   was   to lunch   and   hear
             upon a time   he went

zuen **Bikarioa**   **eta**   **neskamea**   **sukaldean**   **hizketan**
did   Vicar   and   maid   in the kitchen   talking

ari   **zirela,**   **eta**   **bi** **amuarrain** **handienak**
-ing   they were   and   two   trout   (the) biggest
                                                  the biggest two trout

gaberako
for (evening) dinner

gordetzea erabaki zutela.
to keep   decided   that they had

Pernandok   ez entzun   egin   zuen,   eta
Pernando   not hear   (intentional) did   and
                        pretended not to hear

ezer   igarri ez   balu   bezala
anything notice not if he had   as
    as if he hadn't noticed anything

bazkari-tokira bildu zan.
dining-room   join   was
he joined the dining room

Bazkarietan   hasi   dira,   amuarrainak   ekarri
Lunch at   start   they have   the trouts   bring

dituzte,   eta   Pernandok   hartzen   du   bat,
they have them   and   Pernando   take (it)   he does   one

heltzen   dio   isatsetik,   buruz-behera jartzen du,
hold (it)   he does   from the tail   upside-down   put (it) does

belarriondora badarama,   eta   han   dabilke   batean
ear-beside-to   carries   and there moving   in one

gora,   bestean   bera,   aro   berean,   begiekin,
up   another in   itself   moment   at the same   with (his) eyes
                                at the same time

ahoarekin   eta sudurrarekin imintzio mota guztiak
with (the) mouth and   nose with   gesture   types   all
                     with his nose   all kinds of gestures

egiten dituela.
doing   that he is (to them)

Bikarioak, harriturik, galdetzen dio:
(The) Vicar surprised   ask   he does to him

—Baina,   Pernando: zer   esan nahi dute   orain
But   Pernando   what   say want they do   now
                                          do they mean

darabilzkizun   sorgin-hantzeko katramil horiek?
(that) you are handling   witch-like   tricks   those
those weird movements you're making

Ez   zion Pernandok lehenbizikoan erantzun, baina
Not   did Pernando   at first   answer   but

Errektoreak jarraitu zion bere galdeketari, eta ona,
Rector   continue did his questioning   and good
the priest

azkenik, Pernandok   zer   erantzun zuen:
finally   Pernando   something answer   did

—Hara jauna: Ameriketan aire   batzuek baditut,
There   sir   In America relatives some   I have them
Well look   I have some relatives in America

eta denbora asko da beren berririk ez detela. Nola
and time much is their news not have-not As
it's been a long time since I got news from them

arrai hauek uretan ibiltzen direnak diren,
fish these in the water move those that are that are
these fish live in the water (emphasis)

galdetzen nion ia haien berririk ote zekiten.
ask I did whether their news perhaps they knew
I asked of them

—Eta, zer esan dizu?
And what say to you they have

—Esan dit, alegia, hauek gaztetxoak,
Say it has to me that is to say these youngsters

txikitxoak direla oraindik eta urruti haietara
little ones that they are still and far to those places

iritsi gabeak direla. Baina, sukaldeko armarioan
arrive without are-that But (the) kitchen of cabinet-in
haven't been there

handiagoak, zaharragoak egon behar dutela, eta
bigger ones older ones be must that they do and
they must be

beraiei galdetzeko. Haiek zer edo zer
to them to ask They something or something
other

jakin lezatekela.
know   might

Errektoreak,   algaraz   lehertzeko   zorian
Rector   laughter-with to burst-in order to   edge-in
The priest   bursting with laughter   on the verge

dio:
he does
says

—Arraina!   Usain hori ere hartu duzu?   Zelebrea
The fish!   Smell   that also   take   do you   Peculiar
                      Did you smell it?

zera.
that

Eta   neskameari handiena   ekartzeko   otu
And   (the) maid to (the) biggest to bring-in order to to think of
          (dative)   intends

egiten dio.
makes   does to her

Neskame maltzurrak   ordea,   handiena   sukaldean
(The) maid   sly   however   (the) largest in the kitchen
      The cunning maid

utzi eta bigarrena   ekartzen du.
left   and the second one   bring   (she) does it

Baina, Pernandok igarri zuen neskamearen jokua,
But / Pernando / notice / he did / (the) maid's / trick

ta lehen bezela, amuarrainari isatsetik heldu eta
and / (the) first / like / to the trout / from the tail / held / and
like before

lehengo matrakeriak berak egiten hasi zan.
earlier / tricks / himself / doing / start / he was
(archaic of zen)

Bikarioak dio orduan:
Vicar / does to him / then
says to him

—Horra non dezun amuarrain zaharra eta
There / where / that you have / trout / old / and
See / the old trout

handi askoa; zer esaten dizu horrek?
big / enough / what / saying / to you / that

—Bai, honek zerbaiten susmurra badu; bainan
Yes / this one / of something / (a) suspicion / does have / but

guztia ondo ez dakiela, dio. Guztia ondo
everything / well / not / knows not / it says him / Everything / well

dakiena, oraindik armarioan omen dago,
the one who knows / still / in the cupboard / allegedly / is

eta harri galdetzeko.
and to him to ask in order to
    we should ask him

Bikarioak deitzen dio orduan neskameari
(The) vicar calling does to her then maid to
                                (dative)

esanaz:
saying

—Emakumea: neronek jango ez badut ere, ekarri
Woman I myself eat not if I do even bring
          even if I'm not going to eat it

zaioz Pernandori amuarrain handiena
to him to Pernando (the) trout largest
(polite command)

Ameriketako berriak sustraitik jakin ditzan.
America from news from the root know that he may
the news from America thoroughly that he may know

Ala dio neskameak:
So says to (her) (the) maid

—Bikario jauna: ez dakit Ameriketako berriak
Vicar sir not I know (if) American from news
                         news from America

sustraitik jakingo dituen, baina
from the root will know that he will but
thoroughly he will know

gure amuarrain ederrak   sustraitik   jango dituela,
our   trout   beautiful   from the root   eat   that he will
　　our beautiful trout   thoroughly   he will eat

bai.
yes
indeed

Ekarri   dute   azkenean,   amuarrain handi   ura,
Bring   they have   in the end   (the) trout   big   that one
　　　　　　　　　　that big trout

eta sorgin-galderak   egin   ondoren, gure Pernando
and   witch-questions   to do   after   our   Pernando
　　the witchcraft   (emphasis)

bapo   jaten hasi da.
very well   eating   start   he has
heartily

Eta Erretoreak   galdetzen dio:
And   the Rector   asking   does to him
　　the Priest

—Azkeneko   orrek,   zer esan   dizu   ba?
Last one   that one   what   say   it to you   so
　　　　　　　　　then

—Ah!   Oso   ondo   dirala;   urte bete barru
Ah   Very   well   that they are   year   full   within
　　　　they are doing   in a year

hona   etortzeko   asmoa   dutela;   aiek
toward here   to come   intention   that they have   they
　　　　　　　(far away)

etortzean,
when they come

Amezketako
(the) Amezketa of

Erretorea
Rector
priest

ondo izango dala; ni orain bapo nagola ta
well / will be / that he is / I / now / very well / that I am / and
will be well / / / / satisfied

amorraiak on egin dezaidatela.
(the) trout / good / do / may they-make
be good for me (too)

HORTZAK ERAKUTSI!...

HORTZAK ERAKUTSI!...
  Teeth   Show

Pernandok eskribauarekin hitz   egin   nahi zuen.
  Pernando   with the scribe   word do(emphasis) want he did
                                           speak   wanted

Bere etxera   joan zen   eta   dan!   dan!   atea
  His   house-to   go he did   and   bam   bam   (the) door
  To his house   he went

jo zuen. Berehala neskamea azaldu zitzaion.
hit he did Also-like that   (the) maid   appear   did to him
  knocked   Immediately

Neskameak,   **nolako   itxura atera**
  Maids   what kind of expression show
                                   the expression that show

deitzen   dutenak,
  calling   those who do
those who are called (up)

halako aurpegia jarri izan oi   dute.
  such   face   put   have (repeat) they do
they tend to put on such a face

Aberats antzekoa bada
Rich · similar · so
If it is like a rich person

aurpegi guzia irribarrez josirik,   **eta**
face · entire · smiling · sewn with   and
their entire face is covered with a smile

tibiribiri, tibiribiro,
nonsense · chattering
chattering away

sortu diren enbusteri guztiak esanaz.
create · do-that · lies · all · saying
saying all the lies that were created

Erdipurdikoa bada, aurpegi hotza, eta
Half-good-one · so · (the) face · cold · and
Someone of average status · (the maids have) the face cold

itzak hotzagoak oraindik.
words · colder · still
even colder

Eta zarpatzar antzekoa denean berriz,
And · rough, unkempt · similar · is-when · again
· like a hobo · when he is · on the other hand

tximinia baino ilunagoko kopetarekin   **eta**
chimney · than · darker · forehead-with   and
with a forehead darker than a chimney

erratza baino latzagoko hitzekin.
broom · than · rougher · with words
rougher than a broom · (the maid will) talk

Hori	neskame	guztiek	jakiten	dute.	Aralargo
That	maid	all	know	they do	Of Aralar
	all maids		they know		(mountain range)

muturretik	herrira	datorren	neskak,
from the edge	to the village	comes-that	girl

bigarren	asterako	inork	erakutsi	gabe
second	week-by	anyone	show	without
by the second week		no one	not showing them	

ikasten	du.
learn	she does
she learns	

Ez	dago	esan	beharrik	zer	itxura	eramango	zuen
Not	there is	say	need	what	looks	will bear	he had
	There is no need to say				reception	would have to bear	

Pernandok	eta	zer	aurpegi	jarriko	zion
Pernando	and	what	face	put (on)	did to him

neskameak.
(the) maidservant

Pernandok,	apal	apal,	galdetu	zion:
Pernando	humble	humble	ask	did to her
	very humble			

—Nagusia	etxean	al	dago?
Master	house-in	(question)	is?
	at home		

Eta   neskameak,   hitz bakoitzean
And   (the) maid   word   each-on
                                     at each word

bi   purrustada eginez:
two   grumble(s)   making
grumbling twice:

—Ez dakit. Jakingo det.
Not   I know Will know   it
              I'll find out

Horrenbesterekin ezkutatu zen.
With that much   hide   she did
   At that   she disappeared

Pernandok igarri zuen zer arrera egiten zioten
Pernando   notice   did what noise   doing they did
                           they were making

etxe hartan, eta ona zer bururatu zitzaion.
house in that and here is what   occur   did to him
  in that house

Berrogei erraldeko behia erosteko haina diru ez
Forty   of coins   cow   to buy   so much money not
    A cow of forty coins

zuen   noski   berekin   izango,   bainan
did   of course with him   have   but

txanpon bakar batzuek musuzapian korapilo batekin
coin   single some   handkerchief in knot   one in
    a few coins

bilduak bazeuzkan.
gathered   he had them
wrapped

Bere   haiek   askatu   eta   zalaparta   ikaragarria
His own those ones to free   and   (a) ruckus   frightening
 He untied these coins of him

ateraz lurrean   bota zituen.
causing ground-on throw he did to them
         he threw them on the ground

Haserre   bizian,   neskamea   bihurtu   zen,   eta   esan
 Angry   life-in   (the) maid   return   did   and   say
              livid

zion:
to him did

—Gizona.   zer **darabiltzu**   zarata burrunbatsu
    Man   what are you doing   noise   thunderous
                  why are you making   a loud noise

horiekin?
with those

—Badakizu   **—erantzun**   **zion**   **Pernandok—**
 You know   answer   did to her   Pernando

diru mordoxka bat   dakart   nagusiarentzat   eta
money   small pile   one   I bring   for the master   and
    a small pile of money   I am bringing

banaken batzuek   erori zaizkit.
a few   some of them   fall   they have to me
   some of them   fell from me

Hori entzun zuenean,   **neskamea,**
That   heard   she-did-when   maid
  When she heard that   the maid

diruak beretzako izan balira bezala oso poztu zen,
money   for herself   be   did   as if   much rejoice did
  as if the money was for her   became very happy

aberatsentzako bezalako aurpegi goxo irritsua
for the rich   like   face   sweet eager
  a sweet, eager face, like (she does) for rich people

jarri zuen, txanponak biltzen lagundu zion, eta,
put on did   coins   gathering helped   did   and
  she put on

gizontxoa, nagusia etxean dago,   **esanaz,**
young man   master   house in   is   saying
  "young man, the master is at home"

eskribauaren aurrera eraman zuen.
  scribe's   forward   bring   him did
brought him to the scribe

Eskribauak esan zion:
(The) scribe   say   did to him
The scribe said to him

—Zer dugu?
What   we have
What is it

Eta Pernandok:
And   Pernando

—Jaio   ginen- eta, hiltzea zor dugu.
To be born we were and   to die debt we have
　We were born   we owe dying

Gero jarraitu zuen Pernandok esanaz:
Then   continue   did   Pernando   saying

—Jauna, zorrak badauzkat,   hartzekoak   ere bai;
　Sir   debts   I do have them   receivables   also   yes
                                        people who owe me

　hartzeko   dauzkatenei
to be collected   to the ones I have
　　to those who owe me

ez   diet   estutasunik eman nahi,   eta
not   I do to them   trouble   give   want   and
　　I don't want to give them hardship

nik zor   dietenak   berriz   estu   narabilte.
　I   debt those who I have   again   tightly they are driving me
　　those who I owe to   meanwhile   they are pressing me

Larritasun honetan,   zer
　Anxiety   this in   what
　In this difficult situation   something

egin   ote   nezaken jakitera etorri naiz.
to do   perhaps   could I   to know   come   I am
　　for to know what to do   I have come

Eskribauak erantzun zion:
Scribes   answer   did
The scribe   replied

—Hori gauza erreza duzu.   **Hartzekoak,**
That   thing   simple   you have it   Receivables
    That's easy for you   Those who owe you

nola nahi dela ere,   **hartu**   **itzazu,**   **eta**
how   want is-that also   take   (polite imperative)   and
   whatever is the case   go and take them

zor   **diezunei,**   **berriz, hortzak erakutsi.**
debt to whom you have   again   teeth   show
   to those you owe   meanwhilebare your teeth

—Beraz   **dirua**   **eskatzen**   **didatenei**
So   money   asking for   to me-who are coming-to those
                        (di-daten-ei)

hortzak erakutsi?
(the) teeth   to show?

—Hori da.
That   is
That's it

—Ederki iruditzen zait. Eta, orain, berorren
Great   seems   to me And   now   your
                        (formal respectful)

nekea zenbat da?
fatigue how much is
effort fee

—Bost pezeta egin ezazu.
Five   peseta   make it you(command)
            (coin)

—Nola?
How
Come again?

—Bost pezeta.
Five   peseta

Pernandok orduan, hortzak erakutsirik, uuu! egin
Pernando   time-in   teeth   showing   growl do
                  then

zion.
did to him

—Zer da ori? —zion garrasika eskribauak.
What is that   did him   shouting   (the) scribe
                        said to him

—Berorrek   erakutsi   didana.
You (formal)   show   to me-is-that which
                                                    did that to me

Hortzak erakutsi.
   Teeth   show
I showed my teeth

Eta nagusi eta neskamea barregarri utzirik,
And   master   and   maid   laughter-worthy leaving
                                              ridiculous

Pernandok etxe hartatik alde egin zuen.
Pernando   house   that-from   side   make   he did
to leave

www.ingramcontent.com/pod-product-compliance
Lightning Source LLC
Chambersburg PA
CBHW071325250626

47159CB00004B/1465

* 9 7 8 1 8 3 4 2 5 1 0 1 1 *